"I don't like leaving you here alone."

She cleared her voice and seemed to push the worry from her expression. "I will be fine. Call me as soon as you can, though."

"I put a gun in your purse that I had in my glove box in the pickup." He saw her glance toward her purse, which she'd dropped on the table in the corner of the bedroom. "It's a point-and-shoot handgun. All you have to do is pull the trigger." He could tell by her expression that she didn't believe she could do that. He hoped she was wrong—should she need to fire it.

"Eleanor, I..." He realized he was going to tell her that he loved her. It was on the tip of his tongue. This woman had stolen his heart. But for so many reasons he couldn't say the words. Not now. Maybe not ever. "Be safe."

SET UP IN THE CITY

New York Times Bestselling Author
B.J. DANIELS

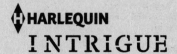

HARLEQUIN
INTRIGUE

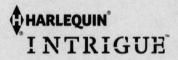

HARLEQUIN®
INTRIGUE™

ISBN-13: 978-1-335-58252-2

Set Up in the City

Harlequin Enterprises ULC
22 Adelaide St. West, 41st Floor
Toronto, Ontario M5H 4E3, Canada
www.Harlequin.com

Printed in U.S.A.

Recycling programs for this product may not exist in your area.

B.J. Daniels is a *New York Times* and *USA TODAY* bestselling author. She wrote her first book after a career as an award-winning newspaper journalist and author of thirty-seven published short stories. She lives in Montana with her husband, Parker, and three springer spaniels. When not writing, she quilts, boats and plays tennis. Contact her at bjdaniels.com, on Facebook or on Twitter, @bjdanielsauthor.

Books by B.J. Daniels

Harlequin Intrigue

A Colt Brothers Investigation

Murder Gone Cold
Sticking to Her Guns
Christmas Ransom
Set Up in the City

Cardwell Ranch: Montana Legacy

Steel Resolve
Iron Will
Ambush before Sunrise
Double Action Deputy
Trouble in Big Timber
Cold Case at Cardwell Ranch

Whitehorse, Montana: The Clementine Sisters

Hard Rustler
Rogue Gunslinger
Rugged Defender

HQN

Montana Justice

Restless Hearts
Heartbreaker
Heart of Gold

Visit the Author Profile page at Harlequin.com.

CAST OF CHARACTERS

Willie Colt—Talk about a fish out of water. The Montana deputy sheriff couldn't have been more out of place on a case in Seattle.

Eleanor "E.L." Shaffer—The high-priced attorney had her life mapped out almost since birth—until Deputy Willie Colt turned it upside down.

Vernon "Spark" Murphy—He liked to blow things up...until this last job when everything went wrong.

Zoey Bertrand—What was she doing in the building Spark had been paid to destroy?

Lowell Carter—He was in love with Zoey Bertrand, but he also owned the mining company that both Spark and Zoey worked for.

Angeline Carter—Her husband's lover was dead. Could she get a divorce fast enough to save her life?

Phillip McNamara—The managing attorney wanted Eleanor Shaffer. If she ever wanted to make partner, she would have to realize he came with the promotion.

Chief Ted Landy—All he needed was some foolish Montana deputy going rogue.

Colt Brothers Investigation—Worried their brother Willie was in trouble, James, Tommy and Davy would do anything they could to help.

Prologue

Vernon "Spark" Murphy couldn't wait to get out of Lonesome, Montana. If the money hadn't been so good… Maybe too good. He tamped down his misgivings about coming back here. Too late now anyway. The job was almost over.

Never do two jobs in the same town. He called it his code. And now he'd broken it. No wonder it made him uneasy. That and the amount he'd been paid. But he also never asked questions, priding himself on always getting the job done.

Now he hurried across the street in the cover of darkness to wait out of harm's way against an abandoned building much like the one he'd just left. It was an odd neighborhood. An old industrial area near what had once been a railyard. The tracks had been removed and the weeds had taken over, giving the whole place an eerie feel that he didn't particularly like on this very dark night.

Counting under his breath, Spark didn't turn around until he reached a safe enough distance out of the way to watch the conclusion of the job. He focused on the three-story brick shell of a building he'd exited only minutes ago. This job was unusual in his line of work because the building was in such bad shape. It made him wonder. He was still counting, reminding himself he wasn't getting paid to wonder or question why.

The first explosion lit the ground floor in a flash of bright orange, streaking across the entire lower level. He looked up to the next floor, still counting. Another flash, this one filling the second floor with a burst of light as it blew out what few windows were still intact on that level.

Even with his reservations, he couldn't help but smile. He did love his line of work. He had always loved explosions and flames. He'd been hypnotized by campfires as a child, so much so that he'd tried to hold the flames. He still had the scars.

Spark felt the growing heat as he looked to the third floor and waited. The entire deserted area was aglow now. He could feel the heat on his face, hear the crackle, smell the fire eating away at anything combustible inside of the structure as it raced across the dry wood floors to rush up the stairs. A faint glow shone even now through the windows of the top floor.

A movement caught his eye. The image of a woman with long dark hair suddenly filled one of the windows. Her features were twisted in raw terror, her scream silent from this distance, her mouth only a gaping, dark hole. Yet he recognized her. *He knew this woman.* She fell against the glass, her wrists bound, her hands frantically beating against the window as if she saw him standing across the street and thought he could—

The flash of bright light rippled across the third floor, engulfing everything in heat and blinding light. The other two floors were already burning. He stared at the window where only moments ago the woman had been standing. She was gone.

Spark heard the too-soon sound of sirens, but he couldn't move. He could hardly draw his next breath. The building had been empty when he'd set his charges, hadn't it? Otherwise, he would have seen her. Unless someone had hidden her, but then she'd somehow gotten free enough to make it to the window? He leaned back against the warm, worn brick of the building, fighting to keep down the meal he'd consumed earlier.

The sound of sirens was growing closer, clearly headed this way. He knew there were no alarms in the building because he always checked. With this abandoned industrial area a good distance from the town of Lonesome, he should have had plenty of time to get away.

His already frantic heart dropped like an anvil. Someone had to have called in the fire even before the first explosion. The same person who'd hidden that woman somewhere in the building so he wouldn't see her, wouldn't even know he'd killed her until the cops pounded on his door?

This was supposed to be a quickie job. In and out. Piece of cake. And the money… He'd been right. The money had been too good on such an old building on the outskirts of this tiny Western town.

Move! He quickly turned away from the flashing lights coming up the street and ducked behind the building. His rig was parked close by. He wasn't worried about getting away since he always planned for just such an unforeseen complication. It was why he was so good at his job.

Until now.

He felt the weight of the woman's death on him, making it hard to think since he had no idea what was going on. But as he drove, one thing became abundantly clear. He'd been set up and he had no idea why. Had it simply been about getting rid of the woman? Or was Spark himself also the target?

Not that it mattered. He'd been in this business long enough to know that even if he avoided capture by the cops, someone more dangerous would be coming for him.

Either way, his life wasn't worth a plugged nickel right now.

Chapter One

Willie Colt was having the best ride of his life on the back of a rank bull with a reputation for maiming cowboys. All Willie had to do was hang on and wait for that eight-second horn to sound.

But just as the horn blew, everything went wrong. He realized his hand was caught in his rigging. Hanging by his arm off the side of the bull, he was being tossed around like a rag doll. Two rodeo clowns were trying to free him and keep the bull's attention as he was dragged across the arena. Then suddenly, the bull stopped, twisted around, horns gleaming in the arena lights as it lowered its head, and—

Willie jerked awake at the sound of an alarm going off. Two nurses came running into the room. One rushed to his bedside, the other shut off the machine next to him as he attempted to sit up. He blinked, part of him still caught in what he realized had been a nightmare from his former career as a bull rider on the rodeo circuit.

"Deputy Colt, you need to calm down," the nurse was saying. "Dr. Bishop is on his way. You're fine."

He doubted that. He was lying in a hospital bed with a bunch of devices attached to him. What the hell was he doing here? "Where am I? How did I—"

"Seattle General Hospital."

He tried to still his raging heart. Moments ago he'd been on a bull about to be gored. He touched the bandage on the back of his head and grimaced. Whatever had happened to him, it wasn't a bull that had done the damage.

"How long have I been here?"

"You were brought in yesterday afternoon."

He'd been here since yesterday? "How did I get here?"

"Ambulance," said the larger and sterner of the two nurses checking his vitals.

His brain felt fuzzy, but two things became clear. He hadn't been riding a bull because he'd retired to become a deputy sheriff—in Lonesome, Montana. He could see his Stetson and his sheriff's department jacket on a nearby chair. And he was in a hospital in Seattle. What the devil was he doing in Seattle and how did he end up in this bed?

"What happened?" He saw the nurses exchange a look.

"I believe you were attacked. Mugged," the smaller, nicer of the two said.

"Mugged?" His head felt filled with cotton. "But what was I doing in Seattle, Washington, in the first place?"

"Picking up an extradited prisoner. At least that's what we were told."

Her grim-faced coworker shot her a look and said, "You received a blow to your head. That's probably why you're a little confused right now. You have a concussion. The doctor will be in shortly if you have any more questions. Just try to remain still."

As they left the room, he lay back against the pillow, wincing, and closed his eyes to ease the killer headache. Slowly, he recalled the drive out to Seattle from the sheriff's office in Lonesome, Montana. The nurse was right. It had been to pick up an extradited arsonist named Vernon, nickname "Spark," Murphy and bring him back to Montana to stand trial for arson—and the death of a young woman who'd died in the explosion and fire he'd started.

Willie, the newest deputy on the force, had gotten the job because no one else wanted it. No one wanted to spend that many hours in a patrol SUV driving all the way to Washington and back—with Spark.

"Trust me," one of the other deputies had told him. "I can promise you that he won't shut up the entire way. You may have to gag him. Seattle can't wait to get rid of him."

They'd all laughed, wishing Willie good luck.

He hadn't known what to believe, but he'd told himself it was no big deal. He liked road trips. Living in Montana, where travel was measured in hours rather than miles, a man had to like driving distances. He remembered thinking he wouldn't mind the company, either.

Willie had known that he wouldn't like the city, though. Born and raised in Lonesome, he liked wide-open places, disliked crowds and hated traffic. Nor was he a fan of water and, after a childhood boating accident, you couldn't get him on a boat.

All that aside, what had happened after he'd arrived in Seattle to land him in the hospital with his head nearly split open? And where could he have gotten mugged? His plan had been to go straight to the cop shop, pick up his felon and head back to Montana as fast as possible.

So, what had gone wrong?

Chapter Two

By the time the doctor stopped by, Willie had remembered a little more of the fifteen-hour drive from Lonesome to Seattle. He'd stayed at a motel in one of the smaller towns outside of the city and gone to the police headquarters in downtown Seattle the next morning.

The traffic had been bumper-to-bumper. He couldn't imagine driving in this every day. In Lonesome, if you had to wait for three cars to go past before you could pull out, then something big was going on in town. There were no stoplights in Lonesome, hardly any stop signs. For miles outside of town it was just an open, two-lane highway as far as the eye could see. Traffic was unheard of until you got to one of the larger cities in the state, and there weren't many of those, either.

He'd found the cop shop with the nav system in his patrol SUV. After signing a few papers, his prisoner had been brought out. He'd only seen Vernon "Spark" Murphy's mug shot, so he'd been surprised when he laid eyes on the slight, five-foot-eight man he was transporting back to Montana. In the photograph, Spark had the look of someone who lived in his mother's basement and played video games all day, only going out at night to light fires and set explosives.

That someone had dressed him up was obvious in the way Vernon was tugging at the collar of his white button-down shirt. His hair had been cut more recently than Willie's own and he wore clothes that looked expensive—and also clearly not his, by the way he moved in them.

If it wasn't for the slight trembling of the man's hands, Vernon almost looked like a man on his way to the office—instead of a man headed for another cell and a murder conviction. Spark climbed into the back of Willie's patrol SUV as if he'd ordered an Uber.

As Willie slid behind the wheel, he glanced in the rearview mirror. His eyes locked through the metal grid with those of the fugitive from justice. "You all right, Vernon?"

"Spark. No one calls me Vernon except lawyers and bill collectors."

"All right, Spark. You might as well settle in for a long ride." He started the engine and didn't hear what the man said. "What was that?"

"It won't be a long ride. We'll never reach the Montana border. They'll kill me before that."

Willie stared at him. "That shows an almost insulting lack of faith in me, Spark."

The arsonist laughed, though the sound held no humor. "You have no idea the people you're dealing with. I didn't, either. Until it was too late." He shook his head. "I told my fancy lawyer that by extraditing me I was being sent to my death. No one listened. But this ride? It's a death sentence—for us both. They'll be worried I'm telling you everything right now. You're just as good as dead and you don't even know it."

"On that positive note," Willie said, and motioned for the cop standing next to the big garage door that they were ready to leave. The deputies back home had been right. Spark was a talker. A depressing one at that. "I can't imagine *that* many people want you dead."

"They're all in on it—the cops, the lawyers, every last one of them. I shouldn't have trusted any of them." He shook his head and nervously pulled at his collar until he finally shrugged out of the suit jacket, ripped off the tie and undid the top buttons on the shirt. "I'm not sure why they sent you to pick me up." His eyes flew to the rearview mirror. "Unless they've already paid you off to help them."

"I'm not on anyone's payroll except the sheriff's department in Lonesome."

"Then your boss must not think much of you."

"Look, believe it or not, I'm going to do my best to make sure nothing happens to you." But Willie couldn't help being a little unnerved.

"Good luck. These people… You won't even see them coming."

"Are we talking about the people who hired you for your last job?"

Spark looked out the side window, clearly not going to answer. He was probably saving that information to make a deal once they reached Lonesome.

As the Seattle officer finally opened the overhead door to let them out of the building, Willie had given him a nod and pulled into the street, anxious to get back to Montana and the open road. He remembered being a little concerned, but not all that worried. His big fear was that Spark was going to keep talking.

After that, things got more than fuzzy. He was guessing that he hadn't gone but a few blocks when they'd been attacked. So where was his patrol SUV? And more to the point, where was Spark, the man he'd not only been paid to protect, but had promised to keep safe?

His head still ached, but Willie was anxious to get out of the hospital. He had to find Spark—if the man was still alive. He kept thinking about how convinced the arsonist had been that he would never reach Montana. Clearly, he'd known what to expect more than Willie had.

But that brought up the question of why someone wanted Spark to never reach Montana.

The attack raised even more questions. Whoever had ambushed them knew the time and place. Where had they gotten that information?

His cell phone rang. He checked it and groaned before he took the call. "Sheriff Henson." He'd never liked Frank Henson, a buddy of the past two sheriffs, who'd made a hobby out of harassing all four of the Colt brothers.

"What the hell is going on out there, Deputy? I just heard that you're in the hospital and that you've lost your prisoner. How in blazes did you do that?"

"I'm fine, but thanks for asking. Just a concussion," Willie said. He took a breath, reminding himself why he took this job, why he still needed it. "We were ambushed. Had to have been an inside job. Don't worry, I'm going to find out what happened and take care of it. If Spark is alive, I'll find him and bring him in."

The sheriff scoffed. "What you need to do is get back here and quit wasting taxpayer money. Let the local law handle it."

"The local law could be who gave the attackers the information about where we would be and when. I was set up and I intend to find out who did it."

"Doesn't sound like you're in any shape to do that."

"Don't worry about me. I've been kicked in the head by bulls that hit harder."

Sheriff Henson swore. "As soon as you're released, I want you back here or you won't have a job. The Seattle police are looking into what happened."

Somehow Willie doubted that.

"I should have known you couldn't handle something as simple as picking up a two-bit arsonist."

He would have argued with the sheriff, but the man had already disconnected. He had a lot of questions about this whole mess. For starters, why would someone want a two-bit arsonist dead, even one who'd killed someone in the last building he'd blown up, before he could stand trial? Because the person who'd hired him worried he would talk? Or was there more to it? Spark had mentioned he'd had a "fancy" lawyer. To Willie that meant high-priced. How had Spark managed that?

There was no doubt that the arsonist had been terrified of being extradited back to Montana for the trial—and with good reason. The ambush to abduct Spark had definitely been planned and executed with help. Willie had to find out who was behind it—and quickly. Spark might still be alive.

He made a call to the police station. He was told that while his patrol SUV had damage—the driver's-side window and the right rear window had been knocked out—it still ran and would be taken to a storage yard. The windows were being replaced as per Sheriff Henson's instructions.

Hanging up, he wondered how he was going to get around until he had wheels. He called the police department and asked to talk to the police officer who'd taken the call on the attack. Fortunately, he was available and filled Willie in what he'd found at the scene—Willie on the ground bleeding and unconscious and the prisoner gone.

"I'd wondered when I saw that the driver's-side window had been knocked out and so had the back seat right-hand passenger-side window," the officer said. "I'd assumed there'd been someone in the back."

"An arsonist I was extraditing."

The officer had called for an ambulance and written up a report.

Willie thanked him and made another call, this one to Colt Brothers Investigation back in Lonesome, Montana. James answered on the third ring. "I need your help," Willie said without preamble.

"Let me put you on speakerphone," his brother said. "Both Tommy and Davy are here."

He quickly filled them in on as much as he could remember that had happened.

"Sounds like you were set up," Davy said right away.

"I need to know why. Could you find out everything you can about Vernon 'Spark' Murphy and what it was about this case that it appears someone doesn't want him to stand trial?"

"Well, you know a woman died in that fire," Tommy said.

"I suspect she's the key," Willie said. "What do we know about her?"

"Very little until they get a DNA match," Davy said. "Otherwise, we might never know who she is or why she was there."

"What if Vernon didn't know she was there? My gut says he didn't and that's why he ran scared. He realized he was set up," Willie said.

"What are you going to do?" James asked.

"Find the people who ambushed us, and hope Vernon is still alive. Either way, I want answers. Sheriff Henson is threatening to fire me if I don't return to Lonesome as soon as I'm released from the hospital."

"How are you feeling?" Tommy asked.

"Angry." His brothers laughed. "I'm getting released right away—no matter what the doctor says. Call me when you have something."

He disconnected and made yet another call as he found his clothing in the closet and began to dress. Within minutes he had the name of Spark's attorney, E.L. Shafer. He looked up the office address, wondering why the attackers hadn't bothered to take his wallet and his phone. Because all they really wanted was Vernon. They'd probably thought that they'd left Willie for dead. Based on the way his skull felt right now, he knew he was lucky to be alive. If he'd been hit just a little harder...

"What do you think you're doing?" demanded a male voice behind him.

"Leaving," he said as he reached for his Stetson and the sheriff's department canvas jacket. "Thanks for patching me up, Doc, but I have to go."

"I'm not releasing you," the doctor said. "If you walk out of here—"

Willie didn't catch the rest as he left. The clock was ticking—especially for Spark, if still alive. He'd found out that E.L. Shafer had an office downtown with a list of other highfalutin lawyers. He thought about calling but preferred a face-to-face with the man. Fortunately, the office was only a few blocks away.

He arrived at the high-rise, asked what floor E.L. Shafer was on and then headed for the elevator, with the man at the desk calling after him. As he entered the elevator, hit fourteen, he saw the man making a hurried call, either upstairs or for security, or both.

The all-glass interior was impressively furnished with thick carpet, a swift elevator and a great view of Puget Sound, he noticed as he got off on the fourteenth floor.

"Can I help you?" the receptionist asked behind a half-moon desk that gleamed.

"I need to see E.L. Shafer."

The receptionist looked at the time. "I'm sorry, the office is closed. Do you have an appointment?"

"I know Shafer's still here because the security

guard downstairs called up. Tell E.L. that I'm the cop who was taking Vernon Murphy back to Montana when I was almost killed and his client taken. The name's Deputy Willie Colt."

The woman made the call. A few moments later a woman in a suit and high heels came down the hallway. He groaned. How many people was he going to have to go through to see Spark's lawyer? He was losing his patience. If Spark was still alive, he needed to find him, and quickly. Even if he wasn't, Willie had to know who'd set him up and why. Once he knew that, then he'd deal with it.

The clack of her high heels on the polished floor drew closer. He'd been pacing in the reception area, but now stopped to watch the woman approach. She was the kind who could turn a man's head. Classic features, great body, long, amazing legs. All of it tucked compactly into a business suit with a blouse buttoned all the way up, to go with the buttoned-up look on the woman's face.

"Deputy Colt?" she asked as the brunette stopped only a few feet from him. Not a hair in her topknot was out of place. He wondered if she was born this uptight. "I'm afraid—"

"No offense, but I'm not interested in speaking with another of E.L. Shafer's gatekeepers. Tell Mr. Shafer I want to speak with him. *Now.* It's urgent."

Her wolf-gray eyes narrowed. "I'm E.L. Shafer."

He was seldom at a loss for words. *"You're Vernon Murphy's lawyer?"* He couldn't keep the surprise out of his voice even if he'd tried.

"You're surprised because I'm a woman?"

Willie shook his head. "It's not your sex that has me surprised. It's that Spark was able to hire any high-powered lawyer from your firm. But I do question why you in particular?"

Either Spark was a bigger player than he'd been led to believe or something was dead wrong here.

"I'm afraid our offices are closing. If you'd like to make an appointment to return during regular business hours—"

He cut her off. "Unless you want Spark's death on your hands, you will talk to me. *Now.*"

She bristled at his tone, her cheeks reddening slightly beneath her perfectly executed makeup as she slowly turned to the receptionist. "Hold my calls." She barely looked at him as she said, "My office," before she did a one-eighty on her heels and headed back down the hallway, back ramrod straight.

He followed, trying to focus on her perfect twist of mahogany hair and the way it wound at the back of her slim neck instead of her compact, perfectly round behind that was impossible not to notice in that skirt. He'd love to get her in a pair of snug-fitting jeans, he thought—a stray thought that told him he was still suffering from the blow to his head.

E.L. Shafer's office was as luxurious as the rest of the floor. "Please close the door," she said as she took the large leather chair behind the huge teak desk.

He closed the door and glanced around. The woman had a corner office with one hell of a view of the city. On the wall behind her were numerous plaques for one award or degree after another. The carpet under his feet felt four inches deep and the entire place smelled of money.

He shook his head, more convinced than ever that something was suspiciously wrong here. "How was it that Vernon 'Spark' Murphy could afford you?"

"Deputy, do I really have to explain client-attorney privilege to you?"

She was angry. She contained it well, no doubt priding herself on never losing her temper. But there was the slight tightening of her full mouth, the tiniest flare of her nostrils and an almost indiscernible twitch next to her left eye.

Willie believed that anger wasn't a bad thing. Maybe he felt that way because right now he was angry as hell. "Look, Ellie—"

"It's Eleanor, but you can call me Ms. Shafer."

He cocked his head. "Let's try this again. How did you come to represent a man like Spark, a small-time arsonist from a town no one has ever heard of in Montana?"

"Like I said, that is privileged information."

He stepped to her desk, flattened his palms on the smooth-as-a-baby's-behind teak and leaned toward her menacingly. He gave her credit. She didn't flinch; she didn't move an inch. Those gray eyes merely bored into him as if she'd faced down much worse than him.

"Let's cut to the chase. If Spark had walked in off the street, he wouldn't have gotten past your security guard downstairs—let alone to your fourteenth-floor executive suite office. And if he had, you wouldn't be representing him—even if he had enough money to hire you." He took a breath. "So, who paid you to represent him?"

That beautifully classic face turned as cold and hard as marble.

Willie rocked back, shaking his head. She hadn't had him thrown out or arrested, yet. But he wasn't getting anywhere with this ice queen. "Look, this is some messed-up sh—stuff. Vernon said that he would never reach Montana. He was right. I'm assuming he meant whoever hired him for the last job. I'm guessing he begged you not to let him get extradited." Something changed in the granite-hard flint of her gaze.

"The men who attacked me and took him had done this type of thing before," he continued. "They weren't a bunch of his rowdy friends breaking him out of the hoosegow. You understand what I'm staying? Vernon was terrified of being sent back to Montana because he knew the people who hired him would kill him before they'd let him drop a dime on them—let alone ever testify against them. Whoever he feared didn't want him returned. This was a *setup*. They knew the time and the place to attack us. That means that someone in the know told them. Someone in the police department or in *your* office." His gaze met hers and held it in a viselike stare. "So, I'll ask you again. Who hired you? Because I'm betting that's who you told."

Chapter Three

Eleanor knew the moment she spotted the cowboy cop with his ten-gallon hat, butt-hugging jeans and dress boots that Deputy Willie Colt was going to be trouble. She should have gone with her first instinct and let security handle him. Outside her window, the sky began to darken as the long day promised to finally end. If managing partner Phillip McNamara hadn't asked her not to leave until he talked to her, she would have already been gone.

"Excuse me, but you didn't just accuse me of setting up my own client, did you, Deputy?"

He gave her a grin that she suspected made some women melt like expensive chocolate. "If the Jimmy Choo fits," he said, locking eyes with her.

"My shoes are Louboutin."

His laugh eased the tension between them. She'd been ready to have him shown out of the building. But her instincts told her it wouldn't be the last she saw of him. There was another reason she didn't have him thrown out. Something about Vernon Murphy's case had felt off from the start. This cowboy had just pretty much told her the same thing.

She leaned back in her chair, crossed her legs and asked, "Does your brand of charm work back in Montana?"

"About half the time. Look," he said, pulling up a chair, sitting down and leaning toward her. "You seem smart." She raised an eyebrow but said nothing as he continued. "There are apparently those who want to shut Vernon up before he rats them out. They couldn't get to him while he was in jail, so they waited until he was being extradited. They had this planned all along and now they have him. He told me when I picked him up to take him back to Montana that this was going to happen."

"You're saying you lost Mr. Murphy."

He removed his hat and turned his head so she could see the large bandage on the back of his head. "They tried to cave in my skull. I need to find them. Maybe they haven't killed Spark yet. Maybe they have. Either way, I owe them and I need your help."

She opened her mouth to remind him again of attorney-client confidentiality, but he cut her off before she could speak.

"You'll help me *because* you're smart. By now, you realize that whoever wanted Spark won't stop until he ties up all the loose ends. That's right, you are now a loose end. These people figure Spark took one look at those amazing legs of yours and spilled his guts. You think it's an accident you were given him as a client? They figured that if there was anyone Spark would bare his soul to, it would be a good-looking woman with mesmerizing gray eyes tucked nicely into an expensive suit."

"I resent what you're implying, Deputy."

He scoffed at that. "Like I said, you're smart. If you didn't know the score, you do now. The people who took him will think the same thing I did—that Vernon talked to you. That's put a target on your back. Basically, you're screwed."

"You have such a wonderfully blunt way of putting things."

"Lady, you haven't even seen blunt yet. What I'm trying hard to tell you is that your life is in danger. I need you to help me before they come for you. Because quite frankly, you'll be worthless to me once you're dead."

Eleanor rose with a sigh. "I'm sorry, Deputy, your time is up. Since we're being blunt, would you like to leave on your own or be dragged out by security?"

He smiled as he shook his head and gingerly replaced his Stetson on his head of thick dark hair. "Damned shame," he said as he rose from the chair. While not an overly large man, he still seemed to dominate the huge office.

"With or without your help, I'm going to find your client—or the men who took him and are probably torturing him—if not killing him—as we speak. I wonder how much time you have left before they come for you? I really doubt you've dealt with men like these before. But if you should somehow get away from them…"

He reached into his jacket and took out his card.

Leaning over her desk again, he picked up her pen. The movement made her want to draw back, but she held her ground, determined not to let this man intimidate her even as he did. He wrote what she assumed was his cell phone number on the back of the card and tossed it toward her. "Call me. I might be able to get to you before they do. Otherwise, they'll torture what they want out of you before they finish the job. I'd hate to see blood on that fancy suit, let alone that white blouse on such an uptight, buttoned-up woman."

With that he turned and walked out, leaving her door open.

Eleanor stared after him, surprised that she was shaking inside. She didn't like being bullied. It made her angry. Uptight, buttoned-up? She took a deep breath and tried to still her raging pulse. Deputy Willie Colt actually thought he could walk into her office, offend her and use scare tactics on her?

A tone sounded as a message popped up on her monitor screen. Her assistant reminding her about the meeting upstairs.

She glanced at the time and rose, shaking her head as she snatched up his card from her desk. He was a deputy from a place called Lonesome, Montana? She'd never heard of it or him. Another message. This time it was Phillip McNamara. He must be anxious, since he, too, was reminding her of their meeting. Still gripping the card the cowboy had given her, she quickly pocketed it in her suit jacket. Her boss would want to know about Deputy Willie Colt, she thought as she headed for the elevator that would take her to the top floor.

ON THE WAY to the main downtown police station, Willie found a quick mart, bought a bottle of over-the-counter painkillers and took three for his headache. He was beginning to question leaving the hospital. The tablets only slightly took the edge off the pain.

He found himself going over the case more critically than he had when he was assigned the job of picking up the fugitive. Seattle police officer Brian Kemp had arrested Spark after pulling him over for a taillight violation, and had been surprised to find out that there was a BOLO out on the man for arson and murder.

But when Willie asked to see Kemp, he was instead sent to the police chief's office, where a large man with a face and voice like a bulldog sat behind a massive metal desk that took up most of the room.

Police Chief Ted Landry motioned the deputy into a chair, but Willie passed. He walked up to the desk, his headache still pulsing, and demanded, "Who the hell set me up?"

Landry was taken aback for a moment before he growled in a gravelly voice, "What the hell are you insinuating about my department?"

"I'm not insinuating anything. I was set up. Those men who attacked me and took my prisoner knew exactly where I would be and what time."

"Well, they didn't get the information from this office."

"I'll ask them when I find them," Willie said.

"I don't know who you think you are, cowboy, but you have no authority out here. You are way out of your jurisdiction. I asked for a rush job done on replacing the broken windows in your cruiser so you can return to Montana as soon as possible."

"That was quick," he said. "Why the bum's rush out of town?"

The chief scowled. "As I told your boss back in Montana, we'll be handling this case from here on out."

"I've seen the way you handled things so far," Willie said, knowing he'd probably said more than he should have. But he was angry, and his head hurt like hell, and he had a bad feeling that no one was looking for Spark—let alone tracking down the men who'd taken him.

"Pick up your rig when it's ready and go home," Landry said, shoving to his feet threateningly. "Otherwise, I'll have you arrested for interfering in police business. Am I making myself clear, Deputy?"

"Perfectly." Willie turned and walked out. It seemed everyone wanted him to go back to Montana, including his own boss. Like hell he would.

THERE WERE FOUR partners in the office when Eleanor reached the top floor suite. They rose and left, nodding to her as they did so. Whatever had been going on, they didn't look happy. Neither did McNamara, the managing partner. She'd already been intimidated today by a Montana cowboy. Now what?

She was a senior partner in the all-male partners' group. Her suggestion to bring in more female attorneys had been shot down even though her parents had started the firm and always thought she'd be the managing partner one day. McNamara had hinted at a co-managing partnership, but things had been strained between the two of them lately. Which made her anxious. Why did he want to see her?

Phillip McNamara waved her into his office. He was a striking man seven years older than her, with gray at his temples that only added to his good looks. He offered her a chair. Usually, he kept things quick since he preferred her to be adding up billable hours instead of warming one of his office chairs.

He'd been especially abrupt at their meetings since he'd made his feelings for her known and she'd had to tell him that she didn't feel the same way about him.

Now she sat, noticing that he wasn't meeting her gaze.

"Just wanted to keep you up to speed on one of your clients," he said, glancing at his notepad as if to recall the client. She could read the name written on the notepad from where she sat. "Vernon Murphy."

"Is there a problem with his extradition?" she asked, even though Deputy Willie Colt had pretty much already told her the problem.

"No, no, you did a great job. Everything was in order. Unfortunately, he has escaped," the managing partner said. Not quite the story the cowboy had told her. "I really doubt he will contact you, but if he does, let us know at once. We'll take it from there. He hasn't contacted you, has he?"

Eleanor shook her head. She thought of the deputy's card in her jacket pocket.

"Just let me know if he does. Everything else all right with you?"

For just a moment, she thought about mentioning her visitor, but something changed her mind. "Fine."

"You look tired. You should go home."

She said nothing as she rose from the chair, wondering why they hadn't done this over the phone. As she left the room, one of the other partners who'd been in the room earlier returned to McNamara's office, closing the door behind him. When she glanced back, she saw the two having an intense conversation.

About Vernon Murphy? Or about the cowboy cop who'd lost her client? Or something entirely different?

As she returned to her office, she saw that the receptionist had left for the day and her assistant, Christie, had her coat on. Eleanor was surprised she hadn't left already.

"Vernon Murphy is on the line," Christie told her. "He says he has to talk to you. It's urgent."

Her first thought was that the cowboy deputy had been overly dramatic about Vernon's life being in jeopardy if the man was able to make a phone call to his attorney. "I'll take it, Christie. You don't need to stay."

As she heard her leave, Eleanor entered her office, sat down and took the call. "Mr. Murphy," she said without preamble. She thought about McNamara's admonition that she call him at once if she heard from her client. Now she would have to call upstairs before she left tonight—if any of them were still around. She couldn't keep this phone call to herself. But it did make her question what was so important about this alleged arsonist-murderer. *"Mr. Murphy?"*

She heard a groan of pain. Her heart lodged in her

throat even before he spoke in an agonized whisper. "They're coming for you. They think I told you. Get out before they—" There was a horrible shriek before the call ended and then nothing.

From down the hall, she heard the elevator door open with a ding, followed by the sound of heavy footfalls.

Chapter Four

Eleanor replaced the phone with trembling fingers and stood. Her first instinct was to hide. Or run. But there was little place to conceal herself in this fishbowl of an office building, with all the glass. And running? The stairs were at the other end of the hallway. The quickest way off the floor was the elevator.

She stared at her open doorway and tried to breathe as the sound of someone stomping down the hallway grew louder. The emptiness of the entire floor seemed to echo as if she needed reminding how alone she was right now. Maybe McNamara or one of the partners was still upstairs. She felt the deputy's card with his cell phone number in her pocket. Too late for that. Too late as well to find a weapon on her immaculate desk.

Suddenly the bulk of a man filled her doorway. With a swallowed gasp, she felt relief wash over her like a tsunami as Deputy Willie Colt stormed into her office. She'd never thought she'd be so glad to see the roughneck deputy.

He stopped abruptly, his blue eyes taking her in. "What's wrong?" He was moving toward her before she could speak. But it wasn't until he laid one big hand on her shoulder that she let go of the edge of the desk she'd been gripping. He eased her into her chair and hunched down, turning her chair so she was facing him. "What's happened?"

Eleanor swallowed, her years of study and work as a lawyer warning her not to confide in this man. If she was going to tell anyone about the call, it should be McNamara—not this cowboy cop.

"Ellie?"

She didn't correct him. She knew he'd seen her fear. Only moments ago she'd been terrified that whoever had Vernon Murphy had sent someone for her. The cowboy was no fool. He'd known she was in trouble long before she did. Was that why he'd come back? "What are you doing here?" Her voice only slightly betrayed her true emotions.

"I realized that if Spark was still alive and had a chance, he'd contact you," Willie said, those blue eyes narrowing as if he could read her like a book. "You've heard from him, haven't you?"

Something she'd learned even as a child was to follow her instincts. It made her a good lawyer. It made her able to think fast on her feet. She told herself to trust those instincts now. This deputy's story rang true compared to what McNamara had told her upstairs only minutes ago. Not to mention the bandage on the back of his head as even more proof that he'd been telling her the truth.

"Mr. Murphy just called." She cleared her throat, recalling the terror as well as pain she'd heard in his voice and wondering what McNamara would say if she told him about the call.

The deputy met her gaze. "Tell me exactly what he said."

She swallowed as she made a decision that could destroy her career, ruin her life—or save it. "He said, 'They're coming for you. They think I told you. Get out before they—' Then I heard him shriek in what sounded like pain and the call ended."

WILLIE NODDED. This explained the terrified look he'd seen on her face when he'd entered her office. She'd been scared and with good reason. He rose from beside her chair, removed his Stetson and raked a hand through his hair as he turned to look out at the city, twinkling as far as the eye could see. Wasn't this exactly what he'd feared? Whoever took Spark wanted to know not only what he knew—but also whom he'd told. He turned back to study the attorney.

She wasn't as pale as she'd been a few moments ago. But one thing he sensed about her was that she was strong, and that was good, because she was going to need that strength—especially if she didn't do exactly what he told her.

"We need to get out of here." He didn't like all the glass in these offices. Nor did he like feeling trapped up here on the fourteenth floor. "You need to come with me." She didn't know him from Adam, so why would she believe anything he told her? He expected her to put up an argument, but he was ready to throw her over his shoulder and carry her out of there if it came to that.

She hesitated, but only for a moment, then opened her desk drawer. He wasn't surprised when she pulled out her purse. He'd already figured that if she had a weapon in there, she would have had it out before he reached her office.

He saw her look toward her phone on the desk as if thinking she should make a call. The police? Her boss upstairs? But apparently she changed her mind as she stood and walked toward a closet set back in the wall. She withdrew a long coat and hesitated again as if realizing she might not be back here for a while— maybe not ever.

"If it helps," he said, "I'll do everything in my power to keep you safe. You have my word on that."

She met his gaze as she pulled on her coat and then walked past him, her back stiff as a board. "I bet that's what you told Vernon Murphy."

He groaned inwardly, knowing it was true, as he followed her down the hallway toward the elevator. "We need to take the stairs. Do you have some other shoes?" he asked, and looked pointedly at her designer high heels. She gave him a stop-underestimating-me look and turned toward the stairs.

That she was trusting him at all surprised him. But she'd told him about the call, he thought as he followed her. That was progress, right? But then again, she'd been afraid. Once that fear wore off, she'd probably change her mind about him.

As he watched her quickly descend the stairs with

little effort in those impractical shoes, he wondered if he'd met his match. He'd have to watch her closely. She was far from believing him. Somehow, he had to convince her that her best bet was with him.

Good luck with that, he thought. His track record right now wasn't good. He might have been able to keep her safe if he was on his home turf back in Lonesome. But in this city, a crowded, unfamiliar and so far unfriendly environment that was already trying his patience, he wasn't so sure. Spark was the perfect example of how well he could be trusted to keep her safe.

They reached the ground floor. He glanced at the security officer's station that had been manned earlier. It was now empty. Willie's gaze shot to the elevator. Someone had just gotten off on the fourteenth floor— Ellie's floor.

"Had you been expecting anyone to stop by your office?" he asked as he saw her follow his gaze.

"No," she said, a tightness in her voice as he took her arm to hurry them toward the exit. "Stay close to me." He could feel the muscles clench in her arm as he steered her out of the building and onto the dark street.

THE MOMENT THEY hit the street, the night air, redolent with the smell of the Sound, enveloped her. *What was she doing?* Now that they were out of the office, she began to question what she'd just done. Why hadn't she called upstairs? Maybe McNamara was still around. He would have known how to handle this. Hadn't he said as much when he'd told her to call him if she heard from Vernon Murphy?

The deputy still had a tight grasp on her arm and was leading her down the street in the wrong direction. She needed to get her car from the parking garage. Earlier, she'd panicked because the frantic call from Murphy had frightened her. It hadn't helped to see that someone had taken the elevator up to the fourteenth floor... She realized it could have been anyone. It didn't mean— She recalled that she hadn't noticed any security personnel at the desk on their way out. Too many coincidences?

A horn honked somewhere in the steady stream of traffic, making her jump.

Eleanor stopped walking abruptly. Several people had to dodge them on the busy sidewalk. But the deputy didn't let go of her arm. Instead, he turned in front of her so they were facing, inches apart. She saw him look over her shoulder.

"I know what you're thinking," he said.

"You have no idea."

"You can't go back to wherever you live," he said so close to her that she could see the lighter blue flecks in his eyes beneath the thick dark lashes. "You can't go get your car, either. They're probably watching us right now."

He was scaring her, but maybe that was exactly what he wanted. She had no reason to put her faith in him. She couldn't even be sure his version of what had happened to Vernon Murphy was true. She should have called McNamara right after Vernon's call. Or if not him, the police. Just the reminder of her client's shriek of agony and what the men who'd taken him were capable of…

"I need to go to the police," she said, determined to take control of this situation.

He shook his head as he pulled her out of the flow of pedestrians and lowered his voice as he moved even closer. "I already went to the police. If you didn't set up Vernon, then one of them did. They aren't going to help you any more than they helped me. Nor do I believe that they are actively looking for Spark and the men who took him, no matter what they say. I'm your best bet to stay alive. I know you don't believe that right now, but it just happens to be the truth."

In the time she'd been an attorney, she knew that the Seattle police force was overworked, undermanned and underpaid. But was she seriously going to throw in with this cowboy?

"Come on," he said, gripping her arm a little tighter. "Trust me, you don't want to do this on your own. Whoever hired you to represent Vernon threw you to the wolves."

She looked into those blue eyes. Trust him? Did she dare? She thought of McNamara and realized that she trusted anyone more than her boss right now. What choice did she have if the deputy was telling the truth?

"Let's get a drink." He drew her toward the door of a nearby busy pub.

The last thing she wanted was a drink, but she was smart enough to know he wanted to get them off the street. She glanced around as they headed for the bar, but she had no idea who might be after her or what they might look like—or if she was even really in danger.

As the deputy closed the pub door behind them, Eleanor felt a jolt. If someone really wanted her dead, they might even come in the guise of a cowboy cop.

Chapter Five

Willie found a corner at the back of the noisy, crowded pub where he could watch the front door as well as the back entrance near the restrooms. When the waitress came to take their drink orders, he asked for a beer. Ellie ordered something he'd never heard of. She looked nervous, as if ready to sprint to the back door and out of here.

He leaned closer, his lips next to her ear. He caught a whiff of her perfume as he said over the roar of voices, "Whoever hired you to represent Spark is the one who's put your life in danger. Not me." He pulled back to meet her gaze. She did not look convinced. "I'm in the same boat you are, except they already tried to kill me."

A large man came through the back door. He was dressed nicely enough, looking almost too clean-cut, but there was an agitated air about him that struck Willie as wrong. The man was looking toward the front of the pub as if searching for someone. As his head started to turn in their direction, Willie pulled off his Stetson and quickly leaned over in front of Ellie, cupped the back of her head with his free hand and kissed her.

Just when her mouth began to respond and the kiss was starting to get interesting, she jerked back, her right hand coming up fast. Just not fast enough. He caught her arm before she could slap him and then checked the spot where the man had been standing. He was gone.

"What do you think you're—"

He let go of her. "A man came in the back door looking for us."

Her eyes widened in alarm as her gaze shot to the back hallway. As she realized there was no one standing there, her eyes began to narrow.

"He was there. Big guy, hair cropped short, close-set eyes, dressed nice but not quite right." He shrugged. "I acted on instinct. But for a first kiss, it wasn't that bad, was it?" he asked. "Sorry, I was just trying to lighten the mood."

She scowled at him as she moved farther away from him. "I don't believe a word from that mouth of yours." She reached for her purse just as the waitress came with their drinks.

He laid a gentle hand on her arm. "Ellie, have your drink, then we'll decide what to do."

"It's Eleanor," she snapped, but he saw her hesitate as he slid the colorful drink she'd ordered toward her.

"I know you're scared. I am, too," he said quietly. "Just tell me this. Someone at your firm assigned you to Spark's case. Someone you trust?" He saw the answer as her lashes dropped over those Seattle-gray-sky eyes. She took a sip of her drink.

"Are there other female lawyers in the firm?" he

asked. "I'm betting if there are, none of them look like you. Isn't it possible that's why you got the case?"

When she looked up, her eyes darkened with storm clouds. Anger pinched her lips.

He hurriedly raised a hand in surrender. "It's just a theory." He picked up his beer, took a drink, watching the entrances, his mind working. "There had to have been a red flag. You didn't think there was anything strange about the case?" He saw her hesitate and got his answer. "I'm guessing that whoever hired your firm offered too much money for a simple extradition of an arsonist, even one facing homicide charges. Or, someone at your firm has a connection to Spark or the person who did the hiring."

"You can't really believe that everyone in Seattle is part of this," she snapped. "Do you realize how paranoid you sound?" He could see that she was having doubts, and not just about him.

He watched her take another sip of her drink. She didn't look as confident as she had earlier. Was she wondering why she was given the case? Had she been suspicious from the onset?

From the sick look on her face, Willie suspected she was realizing that her boss had done exactly that—thrown her to the wolves.

WILLIE TOOK A long draw on his beer and realized he hadn't eaten anything other than some green gelatin at the hospital. "You hungry?"

The look she shot him was incredulous, as if he'd asked her on a date. Or worse.

He signaled the waitress and ordered an appetizer

plate and another beer. Ellie shook her head, still holding her not even half-finished cocktail. She looked more than ready to leave, but he had a feeling that the man who'd stuck his head in the back door might still be waiting outside. Let him wait a little longer. Willie ordered her another drink. For the moment, they were safe. Once they left this pub, all bets were off.

"Is there somewhere you could stay that no one at work knows about?" he asked.

"I work with attorneys. They can find anyone."

"I hope that's not true." But he suspected it was. "What do you suggest we do then?"

She side-eyed him. *"We?"*

"I'm not going to hold you against your will." He saw her disbelieving look. "I won't kiss you again unless I'm forced to."

"Thank you, I think." Was that just the tiniest of smiles?

"But I'm still your best bet for staying alive." She mugged a face and tipped more of her drink into her mouth. It was a very nice mouth, he noted, and checked his phone so he didn't think about it or the kiss. "I have my three brothers looking into the case back in Lonesome."

She put down her glass. "Your brothers are deputies, too?"

"Colt Brothers Investigation. They're private eyes. My father started the business after quitting the rodeo. We all have pretty much followed in his boot prints."

She considered him for a moment before she picked up her drink and finished it. As she put the glass down, she seemed surprised to see another one waiting for her. The alcohol had taken the edge off her just a smidgen. She picked up the second drink, cupping it in her hands as she said, "So, you're a rodeo cowboy."

"I was a bull rider. I quit to join the sheriff's department. I'm actually looking for my father's killer." He saw her surprise. "It's a long story."

"Now you and your brothers are looking for the men who took Vernon."

He figured all lawyers had to be skeptics. "You can check it out on your phone if you don't believe me. Colt Brothers Investigation. Or just Colt Investigation for when it was only my father."

She put down her drink and dug out her phone. He watched her out of the corner of his eye as he scanned the crowded pub. No sign of the man from earlier, but that didn't mean that another one wouldn't come walking in the front door and neither he nor Ellie would realize it.

By the time the appetizers arrived, she'd put her phone away and picked up her new drink again. "Your father's death was ruled an accident."

He nodded as he helped himself to some food and pushed the platter closer to her. "The sheriff back then was a mite crooked and didn't like my family. My father was working on a case the sheriff didn't want him working on." He shrugged. "My gut tells me it wasn't an accident."

ELEANOR FOUND HERSELF studying the cowboy next to her. There was more to him than she'd first thought. Three brothers in the investigation business. As an only child, she'd always wished for siblings. Now his brothers were working to help him. She envied that kind of loyalty, that kind of family.

She realized that she was starting to relax. Probably just the alcohol. It certainly couldn't have been the cowboy, as charming as he was. Or that kiss, as interesting as it had been. But she was glad to be in a public place surrounded by people. The cowboy was convincing. Still, she would be a fool not to have doubts about him.

Since she'd had a yogurt at her desk and that was about it all day, she nibbled on one of the appetizers. The alcohol had mellowed her. What she kept asking herself was how much of this she believed. She knew the only reason she was still sitting here with this cowboy was because of the call she'd earlier received from Vernon Murphy.

She thought of her conversations with her client before today. The deputy had been right. Vernon had begged her not to let Washington extradite him back to Montana. But he wasn't the first client who didn't want to go back to the state where he'd committed the crime. She could guess what information the cowboy wanted from her. That she was here with him already made her feel disloyal to the firm, not to mention what her betrayal meant as a lawyer sworn to uphold client-attorney confidentiality.

"I have to use the restroom." She rose, half expecting him to either try to stop her or go with her. "I won't be long." She started to step away when he reached for her wrist. She turned to look back at him with one of her perfected stares that had worked many times with so-called witnesses on the stand at a trial. "You don't trust me?"

"Probably more than you trust me." He brushed his calloused thumb over the tender skin on the back of her wrist. The look in his eyes suddenly felt dangerous. Her heart responded with a flurry of thumps that hurt her chest. At the same time, heat ran along her veins, warming her blood. He let go. "Be careful."

WILLIE SAT DEBATING as he watched her walk away from him. Maybe she was just going to the ladies' room. Maybe she'd come back. He doubted it. She was hard to read. He reminded himself that there was nothing he could do if she took off on her own. The thought made him swear, since he was convinced that she really didn't know what she'd stepped into when she'd taken Spark's case.

His cell phone vibrated in his pocket. He pulled it out and saw that it was the call he'd been waiting for. "I tried to call you earlier, but your phone was off," his brother James told him. "I have information. Spark worked as a blaster for a mining corporation out here in Montana. He was still working as an explosive expert in North Dakota when he took the job in Lonesome. The interesting part is that the mining corporation is based out in Washington, near where you are."

Willie found himself watching the opening to the hallway that led to the restrooms—and the back door— growing more anxious. "That is interesting."

"It gets better. The woman who died in the explosion he set? Her name is Zoey Bertrand, twenty-eight, a former receptionist at Cascade Extraction Corp in Gig Harbor, Washington—the same company Spark works for. There's a chance he knew her."

"Thanks," Willie said, getting to his feet. "Gotta go, will get back to you." He disconnected and headed for the back door. He told himself that there was nothing he could do if the attorney took off on him. But at the same time...

ELEANOR RELIEVED HERSELF. As she stood at the sink minutes later, washing her hands, the doubts surfaced with a vengeance. As an attorney, she wasn't required to consider whether her client was guilty or innocent. All she had to work with was the evidence and the restrictions of the law.

What evidence did she have that Deputy Willie Colt was telling the truth? Had she let his badge persuade her? Or was it his cowboy swagger? Maybe she should call McNamara. She had his cell number. She dried her hands and pulled out her phone, but then changed her mind. She felt confused, and the two cocktails she'd had weren't any help on an almost empty stomach.

Her instincts told her that the cowboy was dangerous. Clearly he was a loose cannon who played by his own rules. Shouldn't she get out of here and go somewhere until she had a better grasp of what was going on? She could go to a friend's if she really believed her life was in danger. Didn't that make more sense?

Worried she'd waited too long to make up her mind, she started to open the restroom door when it flew open. She jumped back, expecting it would be the deputy. A couple of intoxicated young women came in laughing as they rushed past her. A line was forming in the hall with more intoxicated young women all wearing Bachelorette Party T-shirts.

Eleanor had to smile, remembering nights out with her friends, some preceding one of them tying the knot. Her big-city independence made her even more determined to go her own way and figure things out on her own—no matter what the cowboy said.

Once out of the bathroom, she headed down the hall, past the men's lavatory and out the back door to the narrow alley. As the door closed behind her and she stepped out in the darkness, she had a moment of uncertainty. She stood on the wooden steps just outside the door, the sudden quiet almost deafening after the noisy pub.

Before she could step down to alley level, the pub door swung open, knocking her forward. She fought to stay on her heels as she dropped down the few steps to the alley. She spun around, cursing Deputy Willie Colt, whom she expected to see in the doorway.

Her breath caught at the sight of the large man standing in the lighted doorway before the door swung shut behind him. He matched the description the cowboy had given earlier, of the man he said was looking for them. She froze at the sight of him, unable to move even as he pulled on a pair of black gloves.

For those brief seconds, she told herself that the man wasn't after her. The cowboy had just been trying to scare her, maybe hoping to get a kiss.

She started to turn, knowing that once she took a step, she would run. But the man had read her movement. He lunged down the steps, grabbing her arm before she could move. She watched him pull a syringe from his jacket pocket, her pulse rocketing. There was nowhere to run, nothing in the alley she could use to defend herself. Even if she screamed, she doubted she would be heard in the noisy pub.

Her pulse took off like a supersonic jet at Sea Tac. She tried to pull away, but he only held her tighter as he dragged her to him, clearly determined to inject her with whatever was in the syringe.

WILLIE PUSHED HIS way past the line to the women's restroom, stuck his head in the door and called her name. No answer but giggles and smart remarks from all the women inside. He peered under the four stalls to even more squawks from the women. No Louboutin high heels. He swore as he pushed his way back out and started down the hallway to the back door.

Hadn't he known she would run? Why would she trust him? More important, why had he believed her and her steely gray eyes peering at him from behind the dark lashes? No, it had been the feel of her mouth under his that had made him think he could trust her as far as the ladies' room.

Swearing, he shoved open the back door, expecting her to be long gone and only himself to blame if something happened to her.

What he saw chilled his blood to Montana winter ice. A large man was struggling with the attorney. She'd

taken off one of her shoes, using the spiked heel like a
weapon as the man appeared to be trying to inject her
with the syringe in his hand, all the while swearing
profusely.

Willie pulled his weapon. "Police, stop!"

The words had barely left his mouth when the man
let out a cry of pain. He swung around, bringing Ellie
with him. He shoved her. She crashed into Willie on
her way to the ground, blocking him from taking a shot
as the man took off down the alley, turned the corner
and vanished. But not before Willie saw the damage
that had been done to the man's left eye—apparently
by the lethal heel of Ellie's shoe.

He wanted desperately to go after the man, but Ellie
was on the ground—the syringe next to her. If the man
had injected her with something that would kill her—
He holstered his gun and quickly crouched down next
to her. "Did he inject you?"

She shook her head.

"Are you sure?"

"I'm sure," she said as she pulled herself into a sitting position, then to standing by pulling on his arm.
She stood on one shoe and one bare foot as she reached
into her purse to pull out a tissue. He watched her wipe
blood off the heel of the shoe she'd been using to hold
the man off. He could see that her lips were trembling
even as she tried hard not to show how frightened she
was. Or how nauseated by what she'd had to wipe off
her shoe.

He wanted to shake her. Or at least yell at her, telling her what a fool she'd been to try to leave without

him. But as he watched her struggle to put her shoe back on her foot, he couldn't do either. There was no need. Instead, he offered her an arm as she slipped on the expensive heel.

"Can I have one of those tissues?" She didn't question why he wanted it, merely reached into her purse and handed him one. He saw that he didn't have to chastise her for her foolish behavior as she leaned against him for a moment before she straightened and began to dust off her clearly expensive suit. Except for one lone tear on her cheek and a little smeared mascara, she looked like the professional she was. There was no doubt that she was a woman to be reckoned with, he thought as he leaned down and used the tissue to carefully pick up the syringe. He felt a surge of respect for her even as he wanted to throttle her.

"You're sure he didn't prick you with it?" he asked again. She gave him an impatient look before she shook her head. He examined the syringe. "Probably little chance of fingerprints since he was wearing gloves." He considered it a moment longer, then pocketed it. "Got to try to get a print off it anyway."

"I thought you didn't trust the police?"

"I don't. You know any cops you trust?"

Chapter Six

Eleanor considered that for a moment. "I might know one." She'd expected the deputy to lecture her, warn her again about how dangerous this all was. As if she didn't know since she'd been fighting for her life only minutes ago. Maybe he was smart enough to see that his point had been made, she thought.

"We have to get out of here," he said, looking down the alley where the man had disappeared. "The next time he comes after you, he'll bring help." He met her gaze. "He didn't expect you to fight like that." She swallowed, surprised herself.

"We can't take your car and I'm unable to pick up my patrol SUV yet."

She pulled out her phone.

"What are you doing?" he demanded.

"Calling an Uber. One will be here in three minutes. He's picking us up on the other side of the block where there is less traffic this time of the evening."

"An Uber," he repeated. She suspected from his expression that he didn't have the app on his phone. He'd probably never had the need, or Lonesome didn't have Uber service. Did the town even have a stoplight?

They quickly walked down the alley to the other side of the block as a car pulled up. "E.L. Shafer?" the driver asked. She nodded and they climbed into the back of the sedan and the driver took off.

"Where are we going?" the cowboy whispered.

"I had to give him an address. Right now we're headed for Sea Tac. We can pick up a taxi from there or another Uber. The whole idea is not to be followed, right?" she whispered back.

He glanced behind them. "Right." She could feel his gaze return to her.

Eleanor tried to relax. She was safe. At least for the moment. She leaned back into the seat and fought to calm her still thundering pulse. She'd never experienced anything like what had happened in the alley. Although she'd wondered what she would do if she was ever attacked. It was something a woman living in the city thought about occasionally.

"What do you think is in the syringe?" She knew it was still in his jacket pocket. Did he really hope to get prints off it? Or had he been worried that she was mistaken and had been stuck and might need an antidote?

"More than likely a drug to make you more manageable. Whatever it is, it probably wouldn't have been strong enough." Was that something like admiration she saw in his gaze? Or a rebuff because she'd tried to get away from him?

She looked away, shuddering inside at the memory of her heel puncturing the attacker's left eye. They drove in silence. The lawyer in her tried to put together everything that had happened since she was asked to take

Vernon Murphy on as a client. Given what had happened in the alley, there seemed no denying the fact that her client and the deputy weren't the only ones who'd been set up.

As she considered that, she also wondered how much—if anything—to tell the deputy. He was right about one thing. Her life seemed to be in danger. "Vernon didn't tell me who hired him."

He seemed surprised by the admission. "He was probably trying to protect you. Unfortunately, the person who hired him to do the arson job might not believe that."

Eleanor thought of her client, remembering how nervous and afraid he'd been—and with good reason, as it turned out. She could still feel the effects of the two cocktails she'd consumed. She wished now that she'd eaten more of the appetizers he'd ordered.

"Who do you think has Vernon?" she asked.

"Whoever gains the most by him not standing trial."

She thought about that. "If they wanted to get rid of him, why not kill him while he was in the process of destroying the building?"

The cowboy smiled at her. He did have a killer smile. "Too dangerous. Spark knew what he was doing. Whoever hired him didn't, or that person would have done the job himself." He shrugged.

"If he was taken by the person who hired him, then why torture him?"

She saw him consider that and suspected he'd already been asking himself the same question.

"Could be they don't know if he had any contact

with the woman in the building before it blew. Maybe she passed him a message somehow—that's if he even saw her. I don't know. More than likely they didn't expect him to run. I wonder why he did. Makes me think he did see the woman and possibly recognize her. The sheriff's department got the tip even before the building went up in smoke. Instead, he managed to get away and now the person who hired him has no idea who he's talked to and what he's told them." He sighed and looked behind them again.

"Are we being followed?"

"More than likely, but who can tell in this traffic?" He turned back around. "I don't understand why Spark didn't tell the cops out here the name of the man who hired him."

"You asked earlier if there was a Seattle police officer I trusted. Vernon told me that he trusted one of the cops, but that he wouldn't make that mistake again."

She saw from the deputy's surprise that this was news.

"Did he tell you the cop's name?"

She could feel the alcohol humming in her bloodstream. What if the deputy really was the only one looking for the men who'd taken her client? If she ever wanted this to end… "Alex Mattson."

"Then I'm going to have to find Mattson. If he isn't working for the bad guys, then he's probably already dead, since I imagine Vernon has been persuaded to talk by now."

She pulled out her phone, tapped on the keys and

said, "Mattson lives in West Seattle." She looked over at him and lifted a brow in question.

"Maybe you didn't hear me correctly. Mattson might be working with the bad guys. Or he might be dead and the bad guys waiting for us."

"And if he's not working for them and not dead yet? I've met him. I got the impression he was an honest cop."

"What's the address?" He repeated it to the driver, who changed course.

Eleanor felt a rush of adrenaline even as she questioned how getting in deeper was going to get her out of this mess.

"Anything else you want to share?" the cowboy asked close to her ear.

She didn't look at him as she said, "Vernon *did* see the woman. He said she rushed the window." Feeling his surprised stare, she finally looked over at him. "He swore that the building was empty because he was checking it as he set the charges. But just before the top floor exploded, he saw her." She cleared her voice. "He said her wrists were bound together. She was beating on the window, her mouth open as if she was screaming. He figured she'd been secured in the building but had managed to get free and couldn't escape for some reason."

The deputy swore. "There was a piece of burnt bicycle cable still attached to her ankle when her body was found."

Eleanor felt sick at the thought as she watched him studying the traffic behind them again.

She suspected he couldn't tell if they were being

tailed or not. If they were, they could be leading the bad guys right to Alex Mattson's door. She hoped that wasn't the case, but she'd feel responsible if it was.

"Maybe you should call Officer Mattson. He might not even be home."

"You're probably right." She gave him the number and he placed the call. She was half hoping Alex Mattson wouldn't answer the phone, so she was disappointed when the cowboy spoke. "Alex Mattson? This is Deputy Willie Colt from Lonesome, Montana. I was the deputy sent out to take Vernon Murphy back for trial. I'd like to ask you a few questions." He held the phone where she could hear the conversation.

"I don't know anything about Vernon...what did you say his name was? Murphy?" Then, a pause. "This isn't a good time," Alex Mattson barked, and the line went dead.

The deputy looked over at her as the driver said they had reached their destination.

Eleanor felt weak with guilt over everything she'd done since the cowboy had walked into her office. Until she reminded herself that there were still people out there who would torture her apparently and it was the deputy who'd saved her in the alley—certainly not her boss.

Still, she felt as if she was only getting in deeper and with a man she wasn't sure she should be trusting. Yet, as the cowboy had pointed out, he seemed to be her best bet to stay alive right now.

THE COP LIVED in a small bungalow with a freshly mown tiny front yard. Willie had the Uber driver go past the house and drop him a block away. He didn't think they'd been followed.

"Your first Uber ride?" Ellie asked him as he tried to give the driver money. "I have an account. It's all taken care of, including a tip. Don't worry, he'll wait for us."

"There's no Uber in Lonesome," Willie said in his defense. "And I own a truck, so I have my own ride. The rest of the time I drive a patrol SUV."

"Welcome to the twenty-first century," she said, and started to get out, but he stopped her.

Just as he'd suspected, she'd bounced back from the incident in the alley. At least temporarily. He figured it wasn't something anyone could throw off that easily. The trauma of it would probably hit her sometime in the middle of the night when she least expected it. He wondered where they would be then.

Or if they would even still be together. Once he got out of this car, she might tell the driver to take her home.

"You've proven that you have no trouble moving in those high heels and that tight skirt," he said. "So I'm guessing that if things go south with Mattson, you'd probably outrun me back to the Uber. But let's not try out that theory, okay? You need to stay here with the Uber guy and let me handle this. If things do go south, you tell him to take off like a bat out of hell. But not back to your place."

"You call that a plan? If Alex Mattson is dirty and a deputy shows up at his door this time of night… What could possibly go wrong? But if an attorney—"

"If you're suggesting what I think you are, forget

it." He caught the flash of taillights behind them up the block as someone backed out of the garage at the Mattson house and turned in their direction. A moment later the car roared past as if the devil himself was riding shotgun.

"Change of plan," Willie said, and flashed his badge as he asked the driver to follow the car that had just sped past them with a man he suspected was Alex Mattson behind the wheel.

Chapter Seven

Eleanor hated being caught up in something completely out of her control. She'd once tried surfing in Hawaii, on a trip with friends. She'd fallen, tumbling into a wave that wouldn't let her go. She kept tumbling and tumbling, convinced she was going to drown, before the wave spat her out on the beach.

She'd never wanted to feel that helpless ever again. Yet here she was, in a car speeding through the streets, feeling as if she was caught in that same wave. The deputy was leaning forward and giving the driver instructions, complimenting the man on his ability to keep the other vehicle in sight despite traffic. From lane to lane, they rocketed through the night, lights blurring past.

Eleanor told herself that this wasn't happening. This wasn't her life. For so long her every thought as well as most of the hours of the day had been spent at work. Her parents had both been lawyers. She'd wanted to make them proud, and that meant nothing less than taking back the firm they had started, which Phillip McNamara had somehow wrangled from them. She wanted to see her family name up there again, so she'd worked night and day, head down, only that one goal in mind. She would change that all-boys club if it was the last thing she did.

As she hung on in the back seat of the speeding Uber, she could almost hear what her parents would have said if they could see her now. *"What would ever possess you to do something so irrational and dangerous? Why did you even consider leaving your office with such a man? Didn't we teach you to always follow the chain of command? You should have called Phillip. He promised to look after you."*

"Are you all right?" the cowboy asked.

She had no idea how long he'd been studying her. She nodded, shoving away the voices of her parents as the Uber took a hard left, throwing her against the door.

"Stop here," the deputy ordered. In the rearview mirror, she saw that the driver looked exhilarated. She feared he, too, was risking his life and job for this cowboy cop.

"Give me your phone number," the deputy said to her. "I'll text you the address once I know it. We need to know who lives here." He handed her his phone and she keyed in her number before handing it back.

"Terry, our driver, is going to need a big tip," Willie said.

Eleanor could only nod, thinking she would probably never be able to take another Uber again if the driver gave her a bad review. But if she didn't have a job, she wouldn't be going anywhere, would she?

The deputy gave her a warning look. "Stay here," he said, and was out of the car.

"Is he really a cop?" the driver asked as his adrenaline waned. He sounded nervous.

"Believe it or not, he is. Apparently, this is the way they do things back in Montana."

"That explains the hat," the driver said as they both watched the deputy disappear into the darkness toward the house where Alex Mattson was now parked.

Her cell phone rang, startling her. She checked the screen. McNamara? It rang again. Her heart pounded. Should she take it? The driver glanced back at her as it rang yet again.

"It's my boss," she said, staring at the phone again. "I can't imagine why he would be calling at this hour." Actually, she could. She declined the call to let it go to voice mail, hoping that hadn't been a mistake, and waited for a message or voice mail, but one never came.

What had he wanted? Was there news on Vernon? She highly doubted he would call her if there was. She tried to breathe. Where was the cowboy and what did she do if he didn't come back?

That thought only increased her anxiety. There would be only one reason Deputy Willie Colt didn't come back.

Chapter Eight

Alex Mattson's car was parked in front of the garage at 30478 Seabrook Lane. The house was huge in a line of huge houses that overlooked Lake Union. Lights were on behind the drapes of what Willie assumed was the living room. Another light shone from an upstairs room.

He texted the address to Ellie and checked the time. Late enough that Mattson might have had to wake up whoever lived here. It didn't take her long to cross reference the address with the name of the owner of the house in a database her firm subscribed to. She texted back the name. Jonathan Asher.

The name meant nothing to him. Who's that? he texted back, but didn't wait for an answer as he cautiously approached the house.

Standing in the flower bed, doing his best not to trample the flowers, he peered through a narrow gap in the front drapes. The open-concept house allowed him to see all the way from the living room through the kitchen to the back door. He could see two men standing in the kitchen at the island.

Willie guessed the slightly balding, younger man with the paunch was Mattson. He was talking fast, waving his hands, clearly agitated. He appeared upset about something. After Willie's call just minutes before the cop had taken off like a shot from his house to come here?

The older, more distinguished man with his head of white hair filled a glass with something dark and shoved it toward Mattson, who quickly picked it up and drained it.

From this distance, Willie couldn't hear what was being said. He'd have to go around back to get closer to the kitchen. But that meant going through the gate. There was always the chance Jonathan Asher had a dog. Or security.

Before he could decide, Mattson slammed down his empty glass. It appeared that Asher was attempting to calm the man down—and failing. Asher reached into his pocket, pulled out his wallet and handed the cop some bills. Mattson threw them back in his face and turned to leave.

Willie had to scramble to get out of sight as the cop stormed through the house and out the front door to his vehicle. Hiding in the bushes, he watched the man drive off before returning to the flower bed so he could see what was happening in the house.

Just as he'd suspected, Asher was on the phone. He, too, was now talking fast. Willie moved through the shadows to the sidewalk, then leisurely walked back to the waiting Uber and Ellie. All the way, he couldn't imagine what this might have to do with Spark—yet it felt like the arsonist turned killer was the catalyst that had set something much bigger than his own crime into motion.

Willie just had no idea what it was. But until he found out, he and Ellie might not be the only ones in danger.

ELEANOR FELT A wave of relief as she spotted the cowboy coming out of the darkness. She hadn't realized that she'd been holding her breath until the sight of him finally let her breathe again.

The back door swung open and he slid in, bringing the crisp night air with him. "We're going to need a motel," he said to the driver. "Something out of the way and cheap." The driver got the car moving.

As if sensing what she was about to say, the deputy—like a magician—produced with a flourish a long-stemmed red rose, making her wonder where he'd gotten it. "The motel's just for tonight until I can figure out what we do next," he said as he handed her the rose.

We? She stared at the rose, feeling suddenly close to tears. She should have been curled up in her king bed in her apartment working at this hour. The last thing she wanted to do was to spend the night in some cheap motel—let alone with this charming, handsome, loose cannon of a cowboy.

But the memory of Vernon's call and the vile man in the alley with the syringe had her scared as the Uber driver began to work his way back to a commercial part of the city.

The deputy pulled out his phone. "I'm calling Mattson. I suspect he's in over his head and knows it by now. I want to make sure he does. Maybe if we rattle his cage…" He leaned toward her so she could hear, bringing with him his male scent and the warmth of his strong shoulder against hers.

She heard the ringing stop. Alex Mattson had declined the call. It went to voice mail. "It's Deputy Willie Colt. I missed you at your house tonight. Whatever Spark told you, it's going to get you killed if you aren't careful. Seems Jonathan Asher isn't going to be of any help. You have to know that you could be next. Call me when you're ready to talk. Hope you don't wait too long."

Before he could pocket his phone, it rang. "It's Mattson," he said, and took the call.

"How did you get my number?" the cop demanded.

"I need to know what Spark told you and who you told. I suspect you're the one who gave the information to the people who attacked me and abducted him."

"I don't know what you're talking about."

"I know Spark confided in you. But how does Jonathan Asher fit in?"

A few beats, before Mattson said, "Who?"

"The man you visited tonight. Looked like a pretty intense conversation."

Silence. Then a shocked *"You followed me?"*

"I'm a cop, too, remember? I'm going to find out what's going on—hopefully before bodies start stacking up. I'd hate one of them to be yours."

"Are you threatening me?"

"Of course not. I suspect you have enough people

threatening you, am I right? I'm offering to help, starting with you telling me what Spark told you in confidence before it's too late to help him—or you."

Mattson let out a nervous laugh. "Don't call me again or I'll have you arrested." He disconnected.

"What if he goes to the chief of police and tells him that you're threatening him?" Eleanor asked.

The deputy shrugged as he straightened and pocketed his phone. His shoulder moved away from hers, taking the heat and what little comfort it had offered. "I need to find out which side of the law he's on. I don't think he'll have me arrested, which means he's one of the bad guys."

Eleanor stared at him for a moment, then closed her eyes. Her life was out of control. The only way to stop this was with facts, she reminded herself. She opened her eyes and pulled out her phone. "Jonathan Asher is retired," she said as Willie balanced his Stetson on his knee and, leaning closer, watched her fingers moving in a blur on her phone. She tried to ignore his close proximity and the sweet scent of the rose resting next to her thigh on the seat. "Asher apparently made his money in real estate and investments."

"Can you find out if one of those investments was in a mining corporation called Cascade Extraction Corp out of Gig Harbor?"

"That will take longer than this Uber ride, but I'm sure I can," she said as she pocketed her phone, her gaze going to the rose again. He had to have picked it for her out of someone's yard. Asher's? "Are you going to tell me what happened back there?"

He turned to look at her, drawing her attention to him. Even in the dim light coming from the dashboard, she couldn't help but notice how blue his eyes were or how dark his lashes. He had a couple days' growth of stubble. He looked dangerous, like a man on a deadly mission. A man who could not be stopped when he wanted something badly enough. She thought how different he was from any man she'd ever known as her body warmed to the sexy, diamond-in-the-rough cowboy. She blamed those two cocktails she'd had. No more drinking around this man.

She thought he wasn't going to answer, but after a moment it was as if he realized he owed her more than a flower. "I couldn't hear the conversation, but Mattson was worked up about something. Asher was trying to calm him down. I'm not sure he succeeded. He tried to give the cop money, but Mattson threw it back in his face. How all this ties in with Spark—or if it even does—I have no idea."

"But you suspect it does."

He nodded. "Spark confides in Mattson. Spark is taken. After my call, Mattson races over to see Asher late at night, clearly upset."

"How does this mining corporation fit in?"

"I heard from my brother James. Spark works as a blaster, an explosive expert, for Cascade Extraction Corp. The woman who was killed also worked for the same company."

"I don't see arson as the next step in an illustrious career."

"I suspect someone offered him a job on the side

that paid more than blowing up rocks," he said. "If we look into arson cases that involve property owned by the corporation or its subsidiaries, I suspect we'll see a pattern."

"This is the first time Vernon's been arrested for arson," she said.

"He's either been lucky or he's good at the job. Which is probably why he knew he'd been set up and ran the moment he saw the woman at the window."

She frowned. "If Vernon did reveal the name of the person who hired him, and Mattson didn't go to his boss…"

"He might have seen blackmail as more lucrative. But a very dangerous business. I hope he knows what he's doing if that's the case." He shrugged. "Or he could have gone to Asher because he heard that I was coming looking for the men who took Spark—and those behind it." His grin, even in the dark, destabilized her already weakened emotional balance. The man was alluring, especially after everything she'd been through today. He'd saved her life. How did she deal with that, let alone the fact that there was something so appealing about his rough-edged cowboy charm?

She couldn't. Not tonight. "My boss called while you were…picking flowers."

"Is that something he does, call you this late?"

"No." She could see he was waiting to hear what McNamara wanted. "I didn't take the call and he didn't leave a message. Maybe I should have."

"No. If you had, your cell would have pinged and he would have known what neighborhood you were in.

You were smart not to take the call." But she could tell that like her, he wondered what her boss had wanted— and probably suspected it had something to do with Vernon.

"Sounds like they are expecting you to get a call from Spark."

"Can you please call him by his real name?" she snapped.

He looked over at her, his expression softening. "You think Vernon is better?"

"It is his name."

"Fair enough," he said with a nod, his gaze staying on her a little too long for comfort.

She gave the driver an address of a hotel in Seattle. Out of the corner of her eye, she saw the deputy raise a brow. Fortunately for him, he didn't comment. She was tired, dirty and not staying in some out-of-the way cheap motel with this cowboy lounging in a sagging bed next to her. She was taking charge and they would definitely *not* be roughing it.

Chapter Nine

PI James Colt felt as if he'd fallen down a rabbit hole. He stared at the computer screen. Since Willie's call, he'd been following Cascade Extraction Corporation's maze of subsidiaries, divisions and multitudes of holdings.

The mining part of the corporation had been involved in numerous lawsuits and paid millions in penalties for environmental mishaps at their mines. The state of Montana was still involved in several lawsuits over the mining company pulling out and leaving a mess behind.

It was nothing new for Montana, which used to be called the Treasure State. Since the beginning, corrupt companies had come in, ravished the land and left. This corporation seemed to be no different.

"Are you coming to bed?"

He turned to see his beautiful, pregnant wife standing in the doorway. Realizing how late it was, he shut down his computer and rose to go to her. James couldn't believe that Lorelei Wilkins had agreed to marry an ex-rodeo bronc rider turned private investigator. He'd never thought he could get that lucky.

"How's our daughter?"

"Jamie's sound asleep." Lori had insisted on naming her after her father.

"And our son?" he asked as he laid a hand on Lori's swelling belly.

"Growing every day."

He bent to kiss her, drawing her to him. "We should go to bed."

She chuckled. "My thought exactly. What are you working on that has you so engrossed anyway?"

"I'm doing some investigating for Willie."

Lori frowned. "I thought he was out in Washington picking up an arsonist."

"He was. Unfortunately, he was attacked by a couple of men who took his prisoner. Now he's determined to find them and get the man back." He didn't mention that the fugitive might already be dead.

"Is Willie all right?" she asked, studying him, no doubt knowing there was more to the story. There usually was in this business.

"Concussion, but you know how hardheaded he is. The doctor wants to keep him overnight for observation."

"He's in the hospital?" she asked in alarm as they reached their bedroom suite in the house he'd built for her on Colt Ranch.

"Maybe," James said noncommittally, making her groan. "Probably not. By now, he's probably checked himself out."

"Oh, you Colt brothers," she said with a shake of her head. It was a familiar refrain.

WILLIE DIDN'T KNOW what to do with the attorney. He'd all but kidnapped her. But he couldn't keep her. The smart thing to do would be to talk her into visiting some friends in another state until he got to the bottom of what was going on. The problem would be convincing her—even after what had happened in the alley outside the pub.

Also, even if she was agreeable to leaving the city, he had to admit she'd been helpful. He didn't know anything about the city and, worse, he didn't have the resources she did, because the Seattle police weren't offering any help nor was the sheriff back home.

Terry dropped them off in downtown Seattle at an expensive-looking hotel, from what Willie could tell. He shot a look at Ellie. "You can't use a credit card."

"I used to live in the penthouse as a child," she said with a sigh as Terry jumped out to open her door. "I won't use a credit card and I gave our driver a large tip."

"The county will reimburse you," Willie lied as he climbed out and they walked toward the waiting hotel doorman. He'd have to dig into his savings, but he would pay her back.

His cell rang as they entered the lobby. Ellie went straight to the reception desk. He saw that everyone seemed to know her, from the doorman to the clerk behind the desk. As he took the call, Willie tried not to worry that her boss would also know she might come here.

To his surprise, it was the local cop shop letting him know that his patrol SUV could be picked up at the yard in the morning after paying the towing fee. He disconnected with a curse.

"Something wrong?" Ellie asked.

He shook his head. "Everything is great. You did get just one room, right?"

"You still don't trust me?"

"I could ask you the same thing," he said, their gazes locking. She looked as tired and worn out as he felt. But it hadn't dimmed that spark of rebellious determination in those gray eyes of hers. It reminded him of a wolf he'd stumbled across in the middle of a trail some years ago. The wolf wasn't getting off the path. Willie had quickly considered his options before he stepped off and gave the wolf a wide berth. He'd made some mistakes in his life, but he was no fool.

Letting that wolf get the better of him was one of the smart things he'd done. But he wasn't so easy when it came to the buttoned-up attorney. She didn't know the kind of men they were dealing with. He did. There would be no stepping off the trail to appease these men. Things had gone too far. While Willie was looking for them, they would be looking for not only him, but also Ellie. Spark's call to warn her assured him of that.

"I got a suite with two adjoining bedrooms. I think you'll be pleased," she said as she turned on her heels and headed for the elevators.

He saw she still had the rose he'd picked for her from Jonathan Asher's yard. He couldn't help smiling as he followed her.

ELEANOR WATCHED THE cowboy take in the suite she'd gotten for them on the sixteenth floor of the four-star hotel. He'd let out a low whistle even before he'd walked to the balcony to take in the view of Puget Sound. It looked like a photograph from a brochure, complete with one of the late ferries' running lights glittering on the dark water.

"You're just showing off," he said as he turned to look at her.

She chuckled. "Maybe a little. Maybe I just like to pick my own…motels."

He smiled at that. With the night sky behind him, his blue eyes seemed to sparkle. She felt him sizing her up as he slowly removed his Stetson and raked a hand through his hair. It was thick, collar-length and as shiny black against the skyline as the piece of obsidian a friend had sent her from Yellowstone Park. There was no way the man could have been more handsome.

But it was that hint of wild about him that was most appealing. She could tell he probably would have been more comfortable in a tent in the middle of a pine forest. She'd seen that primal look in those blue eyes of his the moment he'd walked into her office. All her instincts had told her to beware and yet here she was alone in a hotel room with him.

She'd faced down criminals before without batting an eyelash, but the intensity of the cowboy's gaze forced her to lower her eyes. "Your room is that way." She pointed to the right as she dropped the two key cards on the counter next to the door. "My door locks. Nothing personal but I want a hot, uninterrupted bath." She pretended she didn't see the slight lift of his eyebrow or the widening of those blue eyes as she turned toward her room. "You can order something to eat for us from room service."

"What would you like?" he asked.

"Surprise me." She didn't need to see his face to know that he was grinning.

"Enjoy your bath." When she turned before closing her door, she saw that he had moved back to the wall of glass and was looking out at the city lights and the dark water. In the reflection, she saw his forehead furrow before he turned away to find the phone and call for room service. She couldn't imagine what he would order for them as she closed and locked the door. She smiled at the thought since she didn't care. She was starved and her life was out of control and had been ever since he'd walked into her life.

Tossing her purse down, she took off her coat. As she did, she saw that she'd missed a text. It was from Phillip McNamara.

You have me worried. Call me.

WILLIE HAD KICKED off his boots, removed his holster and sprawled on the couch after ordering room service and then calling his brother James and filling him in on what little he'd discovered. He found a news station on the television, but there was nothing that he could find about Spark... Vernon. He'd turned it off, worried that he was trying to save a dead man.

He couldn't help but question why he was still in Seattle. It wasn't his job to find Vernon—or the men who'd attacked him and taken his prisoner. If he was smart, he'd return to Lonesome—just as his boss had ordered him.

But how could he? He glanced toward the closed, locked bedroom door and thought about the buttoned-up attorney in the next room, neck-deep in bubbles. He quickly pushed that particular image away. Even as he felt guilty, he told himself that she wasn't his responsibility. He hadn't gotten her involved in this. Her boss had.

But he couldn't convince himself to leave her to her own devices. The man in the alley had been planning to drug her and take her—of that he was certain. What other answer was there? They wanted to know what Vernon had told her.

Nor could he back away from finding Vernon and the men who'd taken him, any more than he could desert Ellie.

There was a knock at the door. He picked up his weapon, tucked it into the back of his jeans and went to the door. Room service. "I can take it from here," he said to the young man, pulling out a few bills to send him on his way.

When he dragged the cart full of food into the room, he saw Ellie come out of her adjoining bedroom wearing nothing it appeared but a large, fluffy robe. What flesh he could see had a rosy-pink glow. Even in the robe she looked untouchable, although there was a lightness to her gray eyes.

"Enjoy your bath?" he asked. She looked away in answer and tugged the sash on her robe tighter around her. "I hope you're hungry," he said, and smiled because she looked like the bath had done wonders for her. He noted that her long hair was still wet. She'd pulled it up in a ponytail. Did this woman ever let her hair down? Not around him, he thought ruefully.

ELEANOR'S STOMACH GROWLED LOUDLY, making Willie laugh as she joined him at the table by the balcony windows. With a flourish, he removed the covers from the food. She couldn't help but laugh when she saw what he'd ordered. Two beautiful fat, juicy-looking beef burgers, two beers and a basket full of thick-cut French fries.

"If you tell me you only eat lettuce, it is over between us," he joked.

She shook her head. "I've been known to eat beef."

He grinned and handed her a plate. "Smart. You never want to tell a Montanan you don't eat beef." They each dove into their meals. She got the feeling he hadn't had much to eat all day, either. The burger was delicious. She indulged on the fries as well, not feeling even a little guilty, although she'd only been able to eat half of the huge burger. She could feel him watching her as she dragged a fat fry through a puddle of ketchup.

"I thought maybe everyone out here ate salmon," he said.

She looked at him. "What's wrong with salmon?"

"Nothing. I just happen to like the rainbow trout I pull out of a stream back home, fried up with potatoes and onions and served with baked beans and homemade bread." He smacked his lips comically and she laughed.

"I'm noticing a fried theme."

"I might have some coleslaw with my trout sometimes."

Eleanor shook her head. "Who does all this cooking? Don't tell me you do this frying yourself."

He raised a brow. "If you're asking who I share my kitchen with, I don't. I never stayed anywhere long enough to get serious about a woman."

"I believe I asked about food, not your love life."

He grinned and shrugged. "Sorry. When I'm home I cook, usually over a Coleman stove outside a tent in the woods. I got sick of fast food on the rodeo circuit." He dropped his gaze to what was left of his fries. She watched him dredge one through his ketchup.

"But now that you're a deputy, sounds like you'll be staying in one place."

"What about you?" he asked before he took a bite of the fry. "Who cooks for you?"

She smiled, knowing what he was really asking. "No one in my kitchen, either." She laughed. "Not even me. I live in a place where I can order anything I want almost any hour of the day."

He shook his head as if in wonder. "I live in a town

that rolls up the sidewalks at eight every weekday night, ten on Saturday. Sunday, after church, most people get a meal at the family restaurant. Chicken-fried steak is its specialty."

"Fried, of course," she said with a laugh.

They ate in companionable silence for a few minutes, Willie finishing off his fries and Eleanor moving hers around the plate.

"You might like Montana," he said, shoving his plate away. "You might even like trout. I suppose you've never had elk or antelope or venison?"

She shook her head. "I tried buffalo. It was okay. I think I prefer beef."

That made him smile. But then his eyes darkened as his gaze locked with hers. She felt her breath catch in her throat at his look.

"You need to leave town until this is over. I'll let you know when it's safe enough for you to come back."

"I thought that was what the chief of police told you to do."

"I'm serious, Eleanor."

It was the first time he'd called her by her name and not the nickname he'd come up with for her. It gave her a strange feeling in the pit of her stomach. She could hear how serious he was. He was trying to tell her that as dangerous as this had been, it was about to get worse.

"You could go out to Lonesome. My brothers and their wives and girlfriend would make sure that you were—"

"I'm not leaving." She rose. "Thank you for dinner,

but you don't need to babysit me. Nor do I want to cramp your style, so you're free to leave and do your own thing." She pulled her robe tighter around her, already missing the teasing comradery between them from only minutes ago as she walked to her open bedroom door. Stopping, she turned to look back at him. "Good night, Willie." Then she stepped in, closing and locking the door behind her.

Her heart pounded and she wasn't even sure why she suddenly felt like crying. She blamed the long, exhausting day, the fear, the lack of control over her life. For a while, they'd merely been a man and woman sharing a meal and conversation. It was so companionable that it had let her forget that her life was in danger—or that Deputy Willie Colt was only here to find the criminal he'd come to Seattle to collect—and then he'd be gone, back to his life out in the wilds of Montana.

WILLIE SWORE UNDER his breath as he picked up the dishes, put them on the trolley and left it out in the hall. As he walked back into the suite, the city twinkled beyond the balcony doors. He'd never felt so much like a fish out of water. To make it worse, he'd dragged Ellie into this.

It didn't matter that she was already neck-deep in this mess before he'd even met her. Still, maybe she was safer anywhere but with him. Going to his room, he left his door partially ajar so he could hear if she decided to take off in the night. As he showered, he had to rein in any thoughts of attorney E.L. Shafer in the next room—let alone that image he couldn't banish of her earlier neck-deep in a bubble bath.

He removed the bandage from the back of his head to wash his hair. After a long shower, the last part purposely ice-cold, he got into bed. He doubted he would be able to sleep a wink—even in a bed that was so soft and high up off the floor that it was like climbing up on a cloud.

He'd left the drapes open, and lying in bed on the sixteenth floor, all he could see was the glow of the city and the glittering water. No stars like back home. He missed the wide-open spaces, the smell of pine and clear streams, and the magnificent show the galaxy put on almost every night above the treetops.

He thought back to everything that had happened since he'd landed in Seattle. He thought of Spark… Vernon and Ellie and what little he'd learned about her. He tried to make sense out of it all but none of it did. Yet.

He must have drifted off, because when he opened his eyes it was morning. He didn't know what to expect as he dressed in his jeans, boots, Western shirt, and picked up his sheriff's department jacket. He had a change of clothing, but it was in his patrol SUV.

Last night he'd taken the syringe out of his pocket. He planned to take it by the cop shop, not that he had much hope of getting prints from it—or the cops helping.

His first thought was that Ellie would be long gone. Even after the scare last night outside the pub, he figured her stubborn, independent streak would have her preferring to be on her own than to stay with him.

So he couldn't help being surprised when she came out of her side of the suite. She was fully dressed in a different suit, white blouse and high heels. She saw his surprise. "I have my ways," she said of the clothing she'd somehow obtained. "Don't worry, I didn't use a charge card. Here." She reached back in her room and came out with a bag brandishing a gaudy logo on it he didn't recognize.

He took the heavy bag as if he expected to find rattlesnakes coiled up inside ready to strike. He peered in. "You bought me clothes?"

"I figured you probably hadn't brought much with you considering that you hadn't planned to stay."

"Ellie—"

"Don't make a big deal out of it."

He held her gaze for a moment. "Thank you, but how did you know my size?"

"I guessed. Try them on and we'll see how accurate I was."

He couldn't help but feel touched. "I've let women undress me before," he joked. "But you're the first I've let dress me." Chuckling, he turned back to his bedroom, but not before he'd seen the flush that had risen to her cheeks.

ELEANOR HAD TO admit that she was definitely out of her realm—not to mention her comfort zone—with this cowboy and the turn of events. She had considered being gone this morning when he woke up. But right or wrong, she felt she was safer with him. She'd never met a man like Willie Colt. There was a coarseness about him, from his stubbled jaw to his rough hands to his language and lifestyle back in Montana. He was nothing like the men she'd grown up with, the men she'd dated. Nothing like her father.

That he'd called her Ellie this morning shouldn't have pleased her as much as it did. If it had been anyone but Willie— She realized that she was no longer thinking of him as the deputy or the cowboy. He was now Willie, another sign that she was in dangerous waters—on more than one front.

"You have a good eye."

She turned to see him standing in his doorway fully dressed again, only this time in the clothing she'd ordered for him. One look at him and she could tell that everything fit, no small task given his broad shoulders and slim hips and that behind that made his jeans sexier than any trousers she'd ever seen on a man.

"Thank you," he said, actually looking a little embarrassed. "But I can't have you dressing me or—"

Or undressing him?

"—paying for expensive hotel rooms, although I have to admit that bed last night was a little piece of heaven."

She nodded, a smile easing from her. "Just as I can't have you taking care of me as if I'm helpless."

"You're far from helpless," he said, holding her gaze. "But as long as you're in danger I can't let you prove just how independent you are." As if he could see that she was about to argue the point, he continued quickly.

"We need to go pick up my patrol SUV, drop off the syringe with the cops and then put you on a flight to somewhere safe. Your choice. I just thought with my family… It has to be a place that no one knows about, especially your boss and his associates."

Eleanor merely looked at him, waiting to see if there was more he wanted to say. "I thought I made myself clear last night. I'm not going anywhere." As he opened his mouth, she held up a hand. "You need my help. Even you should be able to see that."

"*Even* me?"

"As you've made abundantly clear," she continued, "you don't know Seattle. I do. Since going back to my office or my apartment isn't viable, I'd rather take my chances helping you stop these men than having them track me down elsewhere." Her gaze locked with his. "You're apparently my only option."

"I'm…touched," he joked.

She picked up her purse and raincoat. "My boss texted me last night. He's insistent that I call him." She turned then to look at him. "What do you suggest I do? Since I think you might be right about him throwing me to the wolves."

WILLIE HAD BEEN ready to argue that she couldn't stay in Seattle and she especially couldn't stay with him, but her words and the no-nonsense look on her face stopped him. He saw that he could argue with this woman until he was blue in the face, but she wasn't going to change her mind.

She was right. He'd abducted her from her office

yesterday after she'd told him about her phone call from Vernon. He'd saved her life from the man in the alley. Now she was his responsibility, but he knew better than to say that.

Anyway, she was right. He had no idea where he was going or how to get there. He needed her as much as she needed him. It was an odd pairing, no doubt about that. Had he not come to Seattle, their paths would have never crossed. Even if they had, they would have given each other a wide berth—clearly seeing at a glance that they were nothing alike and had nothing in common. But being thrown together, they were now forced to work together to get out of this situation.

"Let's pick up a burner phone," he said, making the decision. "And see what your boss has to say."

She raised an eyebrow as if he was overdoing the precautions. "And if he asks where I am?"

"Tell him you were unexpectedly called away. A sick parent or—"

"He knows that both of my parents are deceased. They started the law firm that he now controls."

Willie picked up the bitterness in her tone. "I'm sorry."

"Phillip McNamara was my father's protégé."

Still, he thought, there was something not quite right there. Not that it mattered in the grand scheme of things right now unless the man was neck-deep in this. "We'll pick up a phone after we get my ride from the pound."

"You aren't worried that we'll be followed?"

"We'll just have to make sure they don't corner us in a dark alley."

She nodded. "No dark alleys. Got it."

He wasn't sure she did. "If you're determined to see this through, then we just need to stay together so—"

"We can protect each other," she said. "That is what you were going to say, wasn't it?"

That wasn't what he was going to say. He thought of the lethal end of her heel. She was a fighter, no doubt about that. But the next time, the men wouldn't be armed with nothing more than a syringe. "Sure," he said, and had to fight the urge to put her shapely butt on the next plane out of town—one way or another.

They caught another Uber to the towing lot. Once in the patrol SUV, Ellie riding shotgun, he made a quick stop at the police station to drop off the syringe. As he drove away, they both kept watching the cars behind them. Would she even know a tail if she saw one? Willie wasn't all that sure he would in this busy city.

He found a drugstore outside of the main downtown. He worried about leaving the patrol SUV for very long, convinced they had been followed from the tow yard. But if a bad cop had wanted to screw around with the rig, he could have already done it.

It didn't take long to get a phone and return to the SUV. As he walked toward the patrol car, he looked around, telling himself he'd recognize the kind of men after them. He didn't see anyone who seemed in the least bit interested in them. Nor anyone like the man who'd jumped Ellie in the alley last night.

But that didn't mean that the two of them hadn't been followed. Or that they weren't being watched. He bent down and inspected the undercarriage of the patrol vehicle. He didn't see a tracking device. Nor did he see explosives. Maybe they hadn't been followed.

As he climbed inside, he thought about Vernon and the men who had taken him. By now they would have gotten whatever information they wanted out of him. Would he have cleared his attorney? Would they have believed him? Was he even still alive?

He handed the phone to Ellie. "Call your boss. Let's see what he wants."

ELEANOR COULDN'T HELP being nervous about the call to Phillip McNamara. She thought about a time when he was sitting at her family's dinner table. Young, intelligent and very hungry for what her father had to offer, Phillip had been the nervous one back then.

Once he'd taken over the firm, he'd changed. Or was she the one who'd changed once she found out that he'd been after more than the firm? He'd promised her she was on track for managing partner when he retired—or co-managing partner before that, but as she prepared the burner phone the cowboy handed her, she knew the offer had come with strings. McNamara had wanted her as part of the deal. Once he'd realized that wasn't going to happen, he quit pretending he'd ever made other promises he wasn't going to keep.

Now she wondered why she'd stayed at the firm as long as she had. Because the firm meant something to her. But maybe giving her the Vernon Murphy extradition case had been McNamara's way of getting rid of her. Had he known there were going to be problems with it? Or had he known the people who hired Vernon to begin with—people who could ruin her reputation and destroy her career, if not kill her? The thought made her angry and less nervous.

She swallowed, her throat dry, as she called the main number at the firm and asked for Phillip McNamara. "It's E.L. Shafer calling." She waited, not wanting to believe that he'd thrown her to the wolves, as the deputy had so succinctly put it. But all indications were that he had.

This phone call would be the deciding factor, she realized. Was she ready to face the truth? She looked over at Willie, knowing that she had already stepped over a line she couldn't recross. Like the minor quakes that often shook the city, Willie rattled her and the solid ground on which she'd believed she'd built a life.

Now, as she waited for McNamara, she feared that in the next few minutes, she was about to destroy that life.

Willie leaned closer so he could hear the conversation as McNamara came on the line.

"Eleanor, where have you been? Your assistant said she hadn't heard from you. Didn't you get my message?"

She took a steadying breath. This was unnerving enough without Willie so close. She tried to think like the composed, confident lawyer she'd been until she met Deputy Willie Colt.

Just from her boss's tone she knew he was alone in his office. He would never have spoken like this in front of the other partners or junior attorneys. Did that mean that his guard was down? Immediately, she decided to go off script, no matter what the deputy had told her to say.

"What's going on, Phil?"

Silence. She hadn't used his first name since she'd told him she didn't share his feelings. He'd become McNamara to her.

"Why don't *you* tell me, Eleanor."

A knot formed in her stomach at his tone at the same time it made her angrier. "Vernon Murphy called me last night right before I left my office."

He let out an exasperated sound. "I thought I told you to call me the moment you heard from him."

She felt Willie a breath away. This was not the way he'd told her to handle the call, but he wasn't trying to stop her. "I was upset. I walked down to that pub you like, you know the one, where you propositioned me, promising me a managing partnership that hinged, as it turned out, on whether or not we were together romantically?"

"Eleanor—"

"As I left the pub, I was attacked by a man who seemed determined to abduct me."

"Are you all right?" His tone didn't carry much sympathy or concern, though.

"Why did you give me the Vernon Murphy case?" The accusation was clear, but he seemed to want to ignore it.

"We don't discuss cases over the phone. Why don't you come up to my office?"

He had to know she wasn't in her office or even in the building. "That's not possible right now. Surely the reason for you giving me this case isn't a secret, is it, Phil?"

McNamara made a distressed sound. "I'm going to have to call you back."

"Before you hang up, I want you to know that I borrowed a phone since my cell phone was lost last night in my struggle with my attacker. I damaged his left eye in case you run across him."

"Eleanor." He dragged the word out with obvious impatience. "You can't think I had anything to do with—"

"What have you gotten me into, Phil?"

His voice sounded strained when he finally spoke. She could imagine him gritting his teeth, his free hand tapping on his large mahogany desk nervously. "I highly doubt the attack on you had anything to do with the case, Eleanor. I certainly wouldn't have put you in such a position. These things happen as a lawyer. I thought you were aware of that."

"Are you forgetting I was raised by two lawyers, the same ones who put you in that chair you're sitting in right now with that great view of the city?"

"I can tell that you're upset. I am, too. But if you're still interested in ever running this firm, we need to meet and discuss this like two rational human beings."

"We could talk about whether or not you knew the time and the place that Vernon Murphy was being extradited." She thought of the man in the alley. "I'm going to get to the truth, Phil. Enjoy your view from that penthouse office because if I'm right about you, you won't be sitting in that chair when I'm done."

Eleanor disconnected and tried to breathe, the phone still gripped in her hand. She felt the deputy's fingers gently pry it free. She sensed his gaze on her, but he seemed to be giving her time to recover.

"You were right," she finally said, breaking the silence. "He fed me to the wolves." She was shaking inside—not with fear, but with fury. "I meant what I said about taking him down."

"Let's nail the SOB's hide to the wall."

She looked over at him. "I like the way you think, Willie."

His grin eased the knot in her stomach from earlier. From the widening of his blue eyes, she saw that he'd also noticed that she was now using his first name. "All we have to do is stay alive," he said, and put the patrol SUV into gear.

Chapter Ten

Willie watched Ellie out of the corner of his eye as he drove. He was waiting for the fury to burn off, afraid that once she realized what she'd done, there would be tears. He wasn't good with tears. Hell, he wasn't good with most things to do with women when there was a problem.

And there was one hell of a problem right now. While he feared that she'd just burned bridges with her career, he was more worried about keeping her alive. He glanced in his rearview mirror. What were all these people doing driving around at this time of the morning? Certainly not going to work. He'd already decided he had to get off this main thoroughfare, even before his phone rang.

He took the first exit and was dumped into a neighborhood. Parking was impossible, he saw at once. He pulled down a side street and stopped in the middle of it to take the call.

"Are you okay?" his brother Tommy asked at Willie's impatient hello.

"Sorry. It's just…everything out here—the traffic, too many people, no parking, and thugs trying to kill us."

"Another day at the office, huh. I found out something that might help. I tracked down Zoey Bertrand's family. She had been having an affair with the head of Cascade Extraction Corp. Seems he has a cozy ten-thousand-square-foot cabin out here in Montana and an even larger home on Vashon Island out there. His name is Lowell Carter."

"Did the family have any idea if the romance had gone sour?"

"They said that the last time Zoey was home they could tell she was upset. She said there were things going on at work that she couldn't talk about. They knew she'd been seeing Lowell and had warned her that because of the age difference—Lowell's in his sixties and married, Zoey was twenty-eight—the affair might not last. They thought maybe she was starting to come to her senses."

"And that's why she's dead?"

"They think it had something to do with the business, something she might have learned, and that she was killed before she could tell someone. They have no idea what it might have been, though."

"Either way, it might explain why Lowell needed to get rid of her. Do we have any idea where Lowell is right now?"

"I drove down to Bitterroot Valley, where the cabin is. I talked to the on-site property caretaker. All I know is that Lowell isn't there."

"Then he could be out here," Willie said. "At least

we have an even stronger connection between the mining company and its owner and Zoey Bertrand—and possible trouble in paradise. It's a start." He wondered where Jonathan Asher fit in—if he did at all.

"I have some good news," Tommy said. "Bella and I are pregnant!"

Willie knew they'd been trying. "Congratulations! That's great news. It makes my day."

"Just take care of yourself, Uncle Willie. We're going to need you. It's twin boys!"

Willie laughed, told him he couldn't be happier, and hung up. As he turned to Ellie, he said, "My brother Tommy and his wife, Bella, are having twin boys." He couldn't help smiling at the good news.

"Congratulations."

His smile waned. "Are you all right?"

She nodded, but he could see that although the fury had passed without tears, it had left her hollowed out.

"We're going to get to the bottom of this. And if you're right about your boss, he's going down."

She nodded again.

"The woman Vernon saw in the window before the explosion? She was having an affair with Lowell Carter, the owner of the mining company she was working for." He told her the rest. The news seemed to perk her up.

"When do we interview Lowell Carter?" she asked, sitting up straighter, that determined look back on her classically beautiful face. The buttoned-up attorney was back and ready to take on the world. She was right. He did need her.

"As soon as you tell me how to get to Gig Harbor—
and out of this neighborhood, wherever we are."

"Doesn't this vehicle have a navigation system?"

"Not one that's worth a damn."

She shook her head. "Fine, I'll get you there."

THE HEADQUARTERS OF the mining company was a
nondescript building on the edge of Gig Harbor, surrounded by pines and old, used equipment. There were
no cars in the small lot or in front of the building.
While not surprised, since his attempts to call the business had all gone to voice mail, he was disappointed
that there didn't seem to be anyone around.

He climbed out and walked to the door, expecting
exactly what he found—the place locked up tight, the
windows dusty. Peering in one of the dirty windows,
he saw that the inside was deserted. No one had been
doing business here for some time.

"Wasted trip," he said as Ellie joined him.

"Not necessarily," she said, opening the metal mail-
box next to the door. She sorted through the flyers and
junk mail for a few minutes before handing him a car
warranty extension offer.

He took it, frowning until he saw the name, Lowell Carter, and what appeared to be a home address on
Vashon Island.

He grinned at her. "Nice job. So, how do we get to
this Vashon Island?" he asked as they walked back to
the patrol SUV.

He saw that she was glancing around just as he was.
He wanted to believe that the bad guys had quit look-

ing for them, which would mean they no longer felt threatened. Which, he feared, could mean that Vernon was dead.

But from what little he knew about bad guys, they usually didn't stop—not until they were stopped. If they hadn't been followed, it was probably that they weren't seen as a threat because they were on the wrong trail. That thought bothered him more than he wanted to admit. What if he was wrong about the people involved with the mining corporation being the culprits?

"We'll take a ferry," she said.

He shot her a look. "What?"

He thought of the ferry he'd seen last night from the hotel room, crossing the huge, dark water of Puget Sound. "We have to go by boat? There must be some other way."

She laughed as if he'd said something funny. "You own a helicopter? Or would you rather swim?" She pulled out her phone and thumbed the keys for a few seconds. "The shortest ferry route is from Fauntleroy Cove. It will take us right to Vashon Heights. The boat ride is only twenty minutes, but it looks like the best time to go would be after the rush hour. There's one at seven twenty-eight p.m."

"In the dark?"

"Ferries have lights." She pocketed her phone. As she did, she turned to him, frowning. "Do you have something against ferries?"

Willie rubbed a hand over his face. He should have picked up a razor at the store earlier. "I've never been on a ferry and don't have much experience with boats in general since falling out of a canoe when I was five and almost drowning."

Out of the corner of his eye, he could see her looking at him as if he was a species she'd never seen before. "You do know how to swim now, though, don't you?" She didn't give him a chance to answer. "Oh, for crying out loud. You can wear a life jacket and if the ferry goes down, I'll save you."

He chuckled. "Thanks, but I'm not counting on that since I doubt you can swim in that skirt."

She made a disagreeable sound. "This from the man wearing a ten-gallon hat and cowboy boots? You'd be amazed how quickly I can get out of this skirt."

"Now, that's something I'd like to see," he said with a grin, and turned back to his driving.

AT THE FERRY, Eleanor suggested they leave his patrol SUV and simply ride over to Vashon as passengers. "According to this address, Lowell Carter doesn't live far from where we depart the ferry. We'll be harder to follow on foot."

Willie nodded, his gaze bright with something close to respect. She turned away, telling herself that looking into those eyes was what had helped turn her life upside down and now had her on the run from possible killers.

"Let's go up on deck," she said once they were on board. "It's a beautiful night." She saw him hesitate. "Easier to save you up there."

He smiled at that and followed her topside. In truth, she needed the fresh air right now. McNamara had texted her as they were boarding: You have no idea what you're involved in. You need to come in.

He was definitely right about that. She didn't have a clue.

She shoved McNamara out of her thoughts and concentrated on what they knew. On the surface it appeared that Lowell Carter had been having an affair with a young woman who worked for him. There were problems, her parents had said. Did that mean he'd broken it off by having her blown up by a demolition expert who also worked for him? Vernon Murphy was that demolition expert, but he'd been abducted and was presumed dead.

If Willie was right, then whoever was behind all of this was afraid of what Vernon had told first police officer Alex Mattson and Eleanor herself as his attorney.

The ferry pulled away from shore, and she hugged herself from the chill as she stood at the railing, staring out at the dark water. There had been a few people up on deck, but now most of them had gone inside. Willie had moved next to her as if to block the wind. Or maybe he wanted to stand this close in case she had to save him should he go into the water.

She could feel his body's warmth, with him pressed against her. They were so close they could have kissed. Did he ever think about that kiss in the pub? Or had it only been a ruse, quickly forgotten? She met his eyes and swallowed. He hadn't forgotten. Her breath caught as he reached over and brushed back a lock of her hair from her eyes.

Her chignon had come loose in the breeze blowing

off the water. As she started to reach up to repair it, he laid a hand on hers and shook his head. He slowly turned her, pulling her close again, as he backed her against him. She felt the heat and the hardness of his body. Closing her eyes, she concentrated on his fingers in her hair, on the bare skin at the base of her neck. His big, calloused hands surprised her with their gentleness as well as their dexterity. Willie Colt was a man of many talents.

She realized that she'd been afraid to move as he finished. It felt good having him behind her, knowing he had her back. It felt too good. She turned, instantly missing the comfort of his nearness as the cold, damp night air hit her. She could hear the chug of the ferry's engines, the slosh of the water as the boat cut through the waves, the steady thrum of her revved-up blood in her ears.

"The boat ride isn't bothering you?" she asked, surprised at the tightness in her throat as the lights of Vashon Island grew brighter.

He shook his head, locking eyes with her for a long moment before he dragged his gaze away and turned to look toward the island. "I worry more about keeping you safe."

His voice was low, his words trying to escape into the wind skimming across the dark water. She attempted to swallow around the lump in her throat, not knowing what to say because there was nothing to say as the ferry began to slow. Looking into the lounge, she tried to see if there were passengers who looked familiar. Was there a killer among them? She didn't recognize anyone. No sign of the man she'd injured last night.

No one looked dangerous, but she knew she could be proved wrong once the ferry docked and those inside prepared to disembark. She hoped this wasn't a mistake, coming out here to confront Lowell Carter in person. Willie had been almost pensive on the ferry ride. Was it his fear of water? Or was he concerned about their safety out here? She couldn't tell which.

He placed his hand, fingers splayed, on her lower back as they left the ferry. They'd let most everyone go on ahead of them. Now there were only a few stragglers at the edge of the shore, people apparently waiting for a ride. None of them seemed to pay her or Willie any mind.

As they walked into Vashon Heights, the streets were still busy with people hurrying home for the night. Willie walked on the outside, keeping her closest to the building side of the sidewalk. She could tell that he was on alert, expecting an attack at any moment.

Eleanor took a shaky breath. She'd felt safe, as if breathing rarefied air before this. She'd worn her attire and her you-don't-want-to-mess-with-me persona like armor. Now that armor had been pierced—and not just by what was happening with the Vernon Murphy case. She glanced over at Deputy Willie Colt, hating that he made her feel vulnerable in so many ways and had her heart beating faster because of it. Now she felt powerless in ways that made her ache.

Willie seemed to have seen through her, like he'd stripped her naked the first time he'd walked into her office. This cowboy with all his jagged edges had been the first man to do that. None of the men she'd dated had been able to evoke the kind of feelings he had, she realized as they wound through the residential streets of Vashon Heights in the deepening darkness. It made her question why the universe had sent him crashing into her life, since he couldn't wait to flee Seattle. Once he finished his job here, he'd be gone.

Only if they both survived, she reminded herself as Willie grabbed her suddenly and pulled her back into the dark shadows of a tall hedge. The kiss fresh on her mind, she thought for sure—

"Stay here," he whispered, and then he was gone.

Chapter Eleven

Willie moved along the hedge, keeping to the deep shadows until he reached a spot where he could step off the sidewalk and not be seen. He waited, hearing nothing but the thump of his own blood circulating. After a few moments, he told himself his instincts had been wrong. No one had followed them.

Then he heard footfalls on concrete, someone moving fast. He pulled his weapon, determined to find out why they were being followed. From up the street came the shine of headlights. A vehicle moving fast.

He crouched down, no longer sure where the attack might be coming from. The driver of the vehicle hit his brakes, coming to a skidding stop only yards from Willie. A window whirred down and a female voice ordered, "Get into this car right now!"

For just an instant, Willie thought the female driver had seen him and was talking to him. But then a sullen figure dragged his feet up the sidewalk, crossed in front of Willie's hiding place and slunk over to the car. "I told you that if I had to come looking for you again—" Willie exhaled. It was just a teenager being berated for not coming home when he'd said he would.

He heard no more as the teen disappeared inside the vehicle and the driver hit the gas, peeling out and leaving rubber tracks as she took off. He stayed hidden for a few more moments to let his heart rate return to near normal before he peered out.

Across the street, a man had come out of hiding. Willie realized that the man had been standing in the shadows between two houses. Willie watched him look around, almost as if he was lost, before he turned back down the street—in the same direction they had come from.

He waited until the man was out of sight before he went to get Ellie where he'd left her. She stepped out at the sight of him. "False alarm," he said as he pulled a dead leaf from her hair.

She gave him a look that told him she'd seen the man across the street and had inferred the same thing he had: they'd been followed. If it hadn't been for the wayward teenager and his angry mother, they might not have seen him tracking them in the dark from the other side of the street.

ELEANOR STILL FELT foolish for her earlier thoughts of their kiss, when their lives were in so much danger. Seeing the man come out of the darkness across the street had brought her back to earth with a thud. Fear had stolen her breath and kept her immobile as she'd waited and prayed for Willie's return.

When she'd seen the man turn back, she'd finally

taken a breath. As Willie appeared she'd wanted to throw herself into his arms. She hadn't, but only by sheer strength of will. She suspected he'd seen how scared she'd been. The cowboy noticed everything. She felt her face heat in the darkness at her earlier stray thoughts. This was not like her. It was annoying and humiliating and distracting, when now more than ever she needed to keep her head.

They stood in the shadows for a few more moments. The man she'd seen didn't come back up the hill in their direction. The night pressed in on them as the ferry left, and the only sounds were doors closing, people talking on their cell phones, music playing as they walked through the wealthy neighborhood. She thought she smelled meat barbecuing as they made their way up the street to Lowell Carter's address.

Like Jonathan Asher's house, this one, too, was impressive, but at least triple the size of Asher's. It had a wrought iron fence with spikes along the top around the property and a wide, matching gate at the entrance. She saw a security camera over the gate.

Glancing at Willie, she knew that he, too, was assessing how they were going to get inside—especially without being seen. That answer came like an unexpected gift as a car pulled up and was buzzed in. The deputy moved quickly to keep the gate from closing and the two of them slipped inside before it clanged shut.

Rather than take the curvy drive up to the house, Willie took her hand and they cut across the wooded lawn. Another set of headlights flashed behind them at the gate and moments later drove in.

"Seems they're having a party," Willie said as they neared the house and saw a valet approach the last car they'd seen arrive.

"Seems so," she said. A couple dressed in suit and gown exited the car and headed up the wide front steps. "Formal attire? I wonder what they're celebrating."

From the front, the massive house appeared to be made of all glass. They could see inside all the way through to the lights on the mainland on the other side of Puget Sound.

"I hate to think what they might be celebrating," Willie said. "Come on, let's go ask them." She hesitated and he added, "All they can do is throw us out."

"Or call the cops." They smiled at each other like conspirators as they walked up to the door and Willie rang the bell.

A staff member answered the door, and no surprise, the uniformed woman's eyes widened at the sight of the cowboy.

"We're here to see Mr. Carter," Willie said as they stepped in, forcing the woman back. "Tell him he'll want to talk to us."

"May I say who—"

"Deputy Willie Colt from Lonesome, Montana. He'll know," Willie said with a wink.

The woman gave a nod of her head, adding, "Wait here." It sounded more like an order than a suggestion.

Eleanor had come to know Willie well enough that she was anticipating a scene. She hated the thought that she might have to call an attorney friend to get them both out of jail as a well-dressed, distinguished-looking older man appeared, his brows furrowed in displeasure.

"You aren't an easy man to get to see," Willie said before Lowell Carter could open his mouth. "We need to talk." He flashed his credentials, strictly for show since he suspected this man knew exactly who he was and that he had no jurisdiction out here in Seattle, let alone on this island.

"I'm afraid you've caught me at an inopportune time, Deputy," Carter said without even glancing at his ID and badge. "We're having a few friends over tonight."

"We didn't come to visit," Willie said. "We're here to talk about Zoey Bertrand."

Carter frowned, as if trying to recall the name.

"Come on, Lowell," he said. "You didn't achieve all of this—" he waved his hand to encompass the house and grounds "—by playing dumb. I want to know why someone abducted my prisoner, Vernon Murphy. And when I find them, I'm going to bring down this whole house of cards. I have a feeling you're going to be under it when it falls. So, if you have nothing to hide, how about you tell me who hired Vernon to get rid of your indiscretion—if not you."

The older man smiled slowly. "Deputy, there must be some mistake, since as you know, you have no jurisdiction out here. All I'd have to do is tell the police chief that you're harassing me—"

"All I'd have to do is tell your wife about Zoey Bertrand," Willie said. "I'd hate to spoil your party, especially with all your close friends here, so maybe you could spare us a few minutes of your...valuable time to talk to us."

"You really aren't threatening me with blackmail, are you, Deputy?"

"Perhaps I can help," Ellie said. "I'm attorney E.L. Shafer. I think it would be to your benefit to speak with us."

Lowell's eyes shifted to her, as if he hadn't noticed her before that moment. His eyes widened in surprise. "I'm familiar with your firm."

Eleanor nodded, hiding her surprise better than Willie was doing. "The deputy here came all the way from Montana to extradite Mr. Murphy, only to be attacked and his prisoner abducted. He is determined not to leave until he finds out who hired Mr. Murphy to commit the act that ended in the death of a young woman who worked for you. I'm sure we can clear this up quickly, especially if you're the one who hired my firm to represent Vernon Murphy, also an employee of yours."

Lowell Carter hesitated but only for a moment as another car drove up. "If you'll follow me to my office," he said, turning on his heel to lead them in the direction away from the noise of the party—and the couple now exiting their vehicle outside.

Willie shot Ellie an appraising look. She merely shrugged and followed Carter down the hallway and into his office. Carter closed the door behind them.

"Let's get something straight," he said as he took

a seat behind his large desk and waved them into the club chairs facing it. "I wasn't even aware that Vernon Murphy worked for my company. I found out when I got a call from the sheriff's department in Lonesome, Montana, telling me that one of my buildings had been destroyed and a woman killed inside." Lowell Carter cleared his voice and looked away for a moment. "When I learned who the woman was…" He shook his head as if he was unable to finish.

"And you didn't question what she was doing inside the building?" Willie demanded. "Or why an employee of yours had blown up your building?"

"Of course I did. I'm not a fool," he said haughtily. "I certainly didn't hire him to destroy one of my buildings, let alone—" his voice broke and he bit his lower lip for a moment "—kill Zoey. I was in love with her. I was planning to get a divorce and marry her. Nor did I hire your firm to represent him," Lowell said to Eleanor. "As far as I'm concerned the man can burn in hell…and as for my wife…" Again his voice broke. "She knows everything now about Zoey and my plans to divorce her."

"And she's good with it?" Willie said, unable to hide his disbelief. "That what you're celebrating tonight with your party? That all's forgiven since Zoey Bertrand is dead?"

"Not that it's any of your business, Deputy," Lowell Carter said indignantly. "But Angeline is still determined to divorce me. I'm attempting to work things out, but I'm not sure we can overcome this… I'm hoping we can."

Eleanor had once thought that she could look into the faces of clients and tell whether they were guilty or innocent. She no longer believed that. Lowell Carter was very convincing, but there was a good chance that he'd gotten rid of his girlfriend. She could have learned something at work that she shouldn't have or he could have just gotten tired of her. Also divorces tended to be expensive and the man clearly had a lot to lose.

"When did your wife learn about your affair and your plans to leave her?" Eleanor asked.

"She learned when I got the call about the explosion and Zoey's death," he said. "I was in no condition to keep it from her after the call. I confessed everything."

"And if she doesn't forgive you?" Willie asked.

"Then she'll divorce me, take half of my holdings, all of our friends and my reputation and my dignity with it," he said. "I deserve to lose everything we built together. It's what I get for falling in love with someone younger than our daughter."

"You sound like a man who is sorry he got caught, not like one who is truly remorseful," Willie said.

Lowell Carter looked close to tears. "I loved Zoey. I would have done anything to be with her. I understand the police are looking into suspects, including a former boyfriend of Zoey's."

"How involved was your wife in the mining business?" Eleanor asked.

The man looked surprised. "Not at all. Angeline took care of our home, our children, not to mention she was the consummate host. She had no interest in business."

"You're that sure she didn't suspect you were having an affair?" she pressed.

"I'm sure. She was happy with the arrangement we had, her taking care of her part, me mine. She took the news badly. I never meant to hurt her. With Zoey gone, I've pretty much lost everything that mattered—except Angeline. I can't lose her, too." Lowell sounded defeated.

"So, you have no idea who hired Vernon Murphy to destroy your building—and kill your girlfriend?" Willie asked. Lowell shook his head. "Would Jonathan Asher have reason to want to destroy your life?"

"Jonathan?" Lowell's brows rose. "I can't imagine why. He invested in numerous businesses of mine."

"How will the divorce affect his investments if your wife goes through with it?" Eleanor asked.

The man frowned. "I hadn't really considered that. If we divorce, I would imagine Angeline will get rid of the mining corporation, selling it off piecemeal to be rid of it and me. So, if anything, Jonathan will be able to buy it all up if he's interested."

"Except for the half you will still own," Willie pointed out.

"I can't afford to buy her out, so whoever picks up her share can pressure me to sell for pennies on the dollar. I'm afraid I'm caught between a rock and a hard place, wouldn't you say, Deputy?"

"Maybe that was someone's plan," Eleanor said.

"Who else would have been affected if you had left your wife for Zoey?"

Lowell seemed to consider that before shaking his head. "Why would anyone go to this much trouble to destroy me?"

It was a good question. Eleanor had one of her own. "You said your wife had considered filing for divorce. May I ask who her attorney is?"

The man was apparently surprised by the question. "I thought you already knew. Phillip McNamara, the managing partner at your firm. My wife contacted him after learning about my...indiscretion, as she is calling it."

The office door opened and a young woman with eyes shaped like Lowell's stuck her head in.

"Sorry to interrupt, but Mother is looking for you."

"Tell her I'll be right there." He rose as the door closed. "I'm afraid that's all I can tell you."

"One more thing," Willie said as he and Eleanor both got up to leave as well. "Do you have personal security, bodyguards? Did one of them have an accident involving his left eye?"

"Just because the man who attacked me works for him doesn't mean Lowell Carter is involved," Eleanor argued as they made their way off the property. "I tend to believe him."

Willie shot her a look. "The man is a confessed adulterer. You don't think he hasn't lied and cheated and maybe even killed to get where he is?"

"I'm just saying I believe him in this case," she said determinedly.

He scoffed. "I'm not buying it. I want to talk to his wife. I got the feeling that she's the one who threw that shindig back there tonight. Who throws a party after finding out your husband was in love with another woman, a much younger woman, and that he was about to leave you?"

"A woman who wants to show the world that she'll survive after the divorce. Otherwise, all her friends would be whispering behind her back about her."

"You don't think they are anyway?"

At the gate, she shrugged. Just as Carter had told them, it swung open before they reached it. "Depends on what all she tells them tonight. They probably already suspect that he's been running around on her—unless he kept all that out in Montana. Still, a woman knows."

Something about the way she said the last made him turn to look at her as they passed through the gate to the street. "Are you speaking from experience?"

She shot him a look, but clamped her lips shut and kept walking.

He surveyed the street. There was less traffic in this pricey neighborhood than there had been earlier. Maybe everyone was at the Carters' party. He didn't see anyone loitering around, but that didn't mean they weren't being watched.

"Are you doing this for Vernon?"

Her question came out of the blue and struck at gut

level. "Do you mean do I hope to save him?" He shook his head. "I suspect he's already dead, so no."

"Then why?" she asked, stopping to stare at him. There was just enough light from the neighborhood lamps that he could see her features. She wasn't the buttoned-up bulldog attorney right now. There was a softness to her that he found equally attractive and unsettling.

"I'm angry and I want justice," he said truthfully, then softened his voice. "But I also want to make sure that you're okay before I can leave Seattle." He didn't admit that protecting her now outweighed his anger and his need for justice. E.L. Shafer had gotten to him in a way that kept him off balance, and he didn't like it. The sooner he finished his business out here and got back to Montana, the better. He preferred his boots on solid, stable ground.

She started walking again, seeming to avoid his gaze. "Does any of this make sense to you?"

He hated to admit that it didn't at this point, but he was more comfortable talking about the case. "What do you make of Angeline hiring your boss to represent her?"

"It makes me suspicious."

"Me, too, especially since he gave you the Vernon Murphy case. Even if he hadn't known that Vernon had worked for Carter's mining corporation, he would know that the destroyed building was his client's husband's—and that the woman killed was her husband's mistress. I suspect your boss is up to his neck in this," he said. "Have you heard from him again?"

She didn't answer fast enough. He swore and stopped walking. "Why didn't you tell me?"

"He texted me to say that I don't know what I'm involved in and I need to come into the office." She turned to look at him. "It's true. I don't know what I'm involved in."

He heard something break in her voice. He'd seen her angry and scared. Right now, she was more vulnerable than he'd ever seen her. "I'm sorry." It was all he could think to say as out of corner of his eye, he saw the lights of a ferry docking at the shore and a handful of people waiting to get off. He didn't see a man with a bandage over one eye, but he still knew they weren't safe. So, how could he promise Ellie that he would solve this or even that he'd protect her? He couldn't, but he realized that he would die trying. He'd come to care about her, making them both vulnerable.

The night breeze teased stray locks from her chignon. She brushed angrily at them as if her hair was just one more thing she'd lost control of because of him. He suspected that her hairdo was a shield, like her buttoned-up-to-the neck blouse, like the look she gave the world from those wolflike gray eyes. *Don't get too close.* He doubted he was the first man she'd held at arm's length.

But right now, he could see that if he reached for her, she would come to him. The question was what would happen once he held her in his arms, felt the supple parts of her against him, let the thought of kissing her again go beyond merely his imagination?

He swore silently. Seeing her vulnerability on this

sultry night, the lights twinkling on the water, the faint scent of her perfume filling his nostrils, and feeling as lost as she looked.

Even as he stepped closer to her, he reminded himself that he'd sworn he wouldn't go down that path, that he couldn't, that there would be no turning back if he did. He reached for her, throwing caution to the wind.

Over her shoulder, he saw a man come off the ferry, hesitate, then head right for Ellie.

Chapter Twelve

"Eleanor?"

Willie had reached for her, his hand brushing her sleeve as he started to draw her to him. She saw her need mirrored in his eyes. Her body leaned toward his, yearning to be in his arms—a place she felt she'd been headed since she met him. She wanted desperately to surrender to it. The thought came with relief, as well as the knowledge that whatever she was feeling was temporary and so she had to be careful. She could get hurt.

Yet, she didn't care. She wanted to feel his arms around her, to relish in the warmth and strength and scent of him. To lay her head on his shoulder and not be afraid.

"Eleanor?"

She hadn't even heard her name being called. But Willie had. She saw his hand, which had reached for her, drop to his weapon. She turned, her disappointment an ache, and recognized the man coming toward her.

Surreptitiously, she touched the deputy's sleeve, signaling him that it was all right.

"Eleanor? *That really is you.* What are you doing

on Vashon?" A tall, blond athletic man, Lionel was dressed in a suit as if he'd come from work. She realized he was probably waiting for his wife to pick him up. He glanced at Willie with interest.

She took a moment, her emotions in free fall. "Lionel, this is a…colleague of mine." Had Lionel walked up only a few minutes later, she would have been in Willie's arms. The ache became agony. "Deputy Willie Colt from Montana."

"Lionel Hayes," he said as he shifted the briefcase to shake hands.

"How do you know Ellie?" Willie asked.

Lionel raised a brow at the nickname as Eleanor groaned inwardly. He shot her an even more questioning look as he said, "How would you describe what we were to each other, *Ellie*?"

"Lionel and I lived together for a while," she said as smoothly as she could manage. "I think I heard you have a son now?"

He brushed a nonexistent blond lock from his forehead, the gold of his wedding ring catching the light. "Joshua. He's almost a year now."

"Congratulations." She looked at where the ferry had finished unloading passengers. "We really need to catch this ferry."

"It was good seeing you." Lionel looked as if he wanted to say more, but Eleanor had taken Willie's arm, drawing him toward the ferry.

As they hurried away, she could feel Lionel's gaze on her back, a burning sensation that made her nauseous.

"Let me guess," Willie said as they boarded. "Things didn't end well with the two of you."

She looked over at the deputy, her practiced stare relaying everything she had to say about Lionel and the past.

"You can tell a lot about a man by his handshake," Willie said. "You can do a hell of a lot better than him."

She couldn't help the laugh that escaped her as they hurried aboard the ferry. Moments later, deckhands began to pull up the walkway in preparation for departure. She moved to the railing, gripping it hard as she refused to look back toward shore.

Willie joined her. But he was smart enough not to say a word as they headed for the mainland.

THEY'D DISEMBARKED AND were almost to his patrol SUV when Willie got a call from his brother Tommy.

"I'm putting this on speakerphone," Tommy said. "James and Davy are here."

He shot Ellie a look as they climbed into his rig. He could tell that his brothers had learned something important. He put his phone on speaker as well. "Let's hear it."

"I talked to Zoey's sister," Tommy said. "It seems that before she hooked up with Lowell Carter, she'd been with a thirty-four-year-old heavy-equipment operator named Kevin Yates. The relationship was off and on—mostly off, the sister said, because of Kevin's temper. Zoey called the cops on him twice after she started seeing Lowell Carter and ended up getting a temporary restraining order against KY, as his buddies call him."

Lowell Carter had mentioned an old boyfriend of Zoey's. "What are you telling me?" Willie asked, knowing there was more.

"I did some checking on KY, and guess what?" Davy said. "He used to work for the same mining company Zoey and Vernon did, near Lonesome and then later near Butte—and at the same time."

"We're assuming the three of them could have known one another." Willie frowned as he looked over at Ellie. "Which means that when Vernon saw the woman in the window, he probably recognized her. Even if he hadn't known why he'd been hired before that, he would have guessed then. It could be another reason he ran."

"I know you like the idea of bringing down the owner of a mining company that pulled out of Montana, leaving a mess behind, but you could be barking up the wrong tree," James said. "Take a look at Zoey Bertrand's former boyfriend. Kevin 'KY' Yates is an abuser with a history of assault. He had been threatening Zoey and he either knew Vernon or had heard of him and what he did. KY could have set up the whole thing."

"Where is he now?" Willie asked.

"That's the thing. He's out your way," Davy said. "He's working at a mine out of Ellensburg—just over the mountain from you. I checked. There's a bar in Ellensburg the miners often frequent. The Shaft."

"Sounds like our kind of place." He looked over at

Ellie. She cocked her head at him as if to say, *Your call.* "We'll pay him a visit."

"We?" James asked.

He met Ellie's gaze. "My colleague and…me." He disconnected, smiling. "We're going to have to get you some real clothes before we go to a place like The Shaft."

"I beg your pardon?"

"Leave it to me." The truth was, he couldn't wait to see her in a pair of tight-fitting jeans. "I think it's time to go shopping."

Before she could put up an argument, he started the patrol SUV. As he did, her cell phone pinged. He watched her check the text she'd gotten, then look up at him.

"It's McNamara again. He insists we meet in person."

ELEANOR SAW MCNAMARA waiting for her at one of the outside tables the next day. A stiff wind brought the scent of rain. Over the city, a bank of dark clouds announced a thunderstorm before the day was over. The approaching storm had chased off late diners apparently. The other outside tables sat empty.

As she approached Phillip, she could see the cup of coffee he hadn't touched. Instead, he kept looking at his phone, as if expecting a call. From her? Had he really thought she wouldn't come? With his other hand, he tapped the table nervously.

Looking up, he saw her and seemed to relax, pushing his phone away. He smiled as if posing for a photo.

There was no warmth in it, though—or in his eyes. She realized he might have gotten her here to fire her. Could he do that? He could. Her father had given him control of the firm. Phillip could do whatever he liked within the all-male firm, which was one reason she was the only female lawyer.

Her parents had liked Phillip, trusted him. Clearly either they hadn't seen beyond the veneer or they were too busy and distracted to look deeper.

She slowed, afraid this had been a mistake even though it had been her idea and had taken some persuading to talk Willie into it. She felt her phone in her pocket. He would be listening and watching. If anything seemed at all hinky, he'd promised to pull her out, so she knew he would be close by.

Keeping her expression blank as if facing a jury, she walked to the table. His smile faded as she took a seat opposite him. The wind tugged at her hair. She brushed back a lock that had come loose and faced him, waiting.

"What are you doing?" he demanded, clearly exasperated with her, but then quickly softened his tone as he saw her stiffen. "I've been worried sick about you, Eleanor. You know I still care about you."

"Is that why you gave me the Vernon Murphy case?"

He groaned. "I had no idea any of this would happen." He looked toward the pub. "Do you want something to—"

"No. Who hired the firm?"

He met her gaze but said nothing.

"Who are you protecting?"

"Client-attorney confidentiality."

She shook her head and started to get to her feet.

"Where are you g— Sit back down. *Please*," he added quickly.

"Tell me what's going on or I'm done." She was still standing, still ready to leave. This had been a waste of time—just like staying with the firm after she'd turned down Phillip's advances. She'd thought she could change it within. She'd been wrong.

"You aren't going to throw your career and your future away over something this trivial." She said nothing. In ten seconds, she was walking. "Angeline Carter wanted my best lawyer. That is you."

She frowned. "I know she came to you about a divorce, but…" She saw his surprise that she knew. She slowly sat down in the chair across from him again. "Why would she hire the firm to represent the man who killed her husband's lover unless… Unless she had hired Vernon to kill Zoey Bertrand and wanted to make sure he never talked."

Phillip shook his head. "I don't know where you get your information, but it's just the opposite. She wanted to know who hired Vernon Murphy and set him up, fearing it was her husband and she might be next."

Eleanor scoffed. "That's ridiculous. Why would he kill his own girlfriend?"

"Because things had gone sour between them, and she'd become a liability."

"How could his wife know that?" she asked.

He looked away for a moment, no doubt uncomfortable with sharing what would have been client-attorney privilege. "She said she didn't know who the woman was that he'd been seeing but she'd been through this kind of thing with him before. Only this time, the affair was ending badly. She'd overheard him on the phone. Apparently, Zoey Bertrand knew things he'd done at one of the mines that could have gotten the mine closed down and him thrown in prison."

Eleanor shook her head. She wasn't buying this.

"She believes her husband got rid of his girlfriend for good and if she tries to divorce him, he'll kill her, too. She said she's had several close calls after contacting me."

This certainly wasn't the story her husband had told them. "Why would he want her dead?"

"Money. Lowell has a ten-million-dollar policy on Angeline and himself. Lowell made no secret of the fact that he was going to marry the woman. He'd purchased her a very expensive emerald-and-diamond ring—which I'm told wasn't found on the body. It's possible that Vernon Murphy took it, since no one believes he didn't know she was tied up in the building before he demolished it."

Eleanor thought of what Vernon had told her about seeing the woman with duct-taped wrists, hands banging on the window, mouth open in a scream. It was more believable than Phillip's story. "Let's pretend this is all true. Whose idea was it to put me on the case?"

He held her gaze for an uncomfortable length of time before he said, "Angeline wanted my best, so I guess it was my idea. I also wanted someone I could trust on it."

"Trust me to what?"

"To tell me everything Vernon told you. You've always been so…professional. I just assumed you would come to me if there was a problem with the case— before you took off with that cowboy cop. I had security check the cameras in the building. Why would you leave with the man?"

She ignored the question. "The men who attacked Deputy Colt weren't Vernon's friends. They wanted something from him. What do you imagine that was?"

"How would I know? Maybe the ring. It's worth a small fortune, according to Angeline. He didn't say anything to you about it?"

She shook her head and waited.

His eyes widened. *"You can't believe I had anything to do with Vernon getting away."*

"Someone tipped them off as to when Vernon was being extradited and where."

"What are you insinuating?"

"That you know more than you're telling me. Why did you really give me the case?"

"Damn it, Eleanor," he said, lowering his voice as he leaned toward her, even though they were alone out in the wind and growing cold. The air grew damper by the minute. "I thought he might confess everything to you. I told you when I gave you the case that I wanted updates. I was only concerned because Lowell Carter was involved and I was representing his wife."

"Wait, Angeline Carter hired you *before* Vernon blew up the building in Lonesome, Montana, and killed her husband's lover?"

"No, not hired me. She knew Lowell was having an affair and she said it felt different this time. She wanted to know what her options were. When the woman was killed in the demolished building and Vernon was caught out here, she wanted to know if her husband had hired him to do it. The case was a simple extradition."

"But it wasn't a simple extradition case and I suspect you knew it."

He groaned, shaking his head as he avoided her gaze. "Did Vernon Murphy tell you who hired him or not?"

"Not." She saw his disappointment, then his distrust.

"You're sure he didn't mention a ring?"

Eleanor thought about what Willie had said about Vernon taking one look at her long legs and unburdening himself. Phillip had obviously thought the same thing when he'd thrown her at Vernon. They were both wrong.

She got to her feet again but paused. "I want to believe that you didn't realize how dangerous this case was when you gave it to me. Or that you weren't the one to tip off the men who took Vernon. Tell me I can trust you."

"Do you really have to ask?" He met her gaze again and she saw such regret in his eyes that it made her heart ache. He *had* loved her. Maybe he thought he still did. But she hadn't loved him and was no longer sure she could trust him or anyone else. Anyone except Deputy Willie Colt.

"I hope now that we've talked, this means you're coming back to work." Phillip sounded impatient with her, as if she was being childish. Was her life still in danger? Willie had tried to send her away so she'd be safe. Why hadn't she gone, if she truly believed she was in danger?

A thought stopped her cold. Was she going along with Willie because she was still scared or because she was starting to enjoy the cowboy's company?

The roar of a car engine and the squeal of tires on pavement made her turn in time to see a dark SUV speeding toward them. As it roared past, she saw a masked man half hanging out the window, a gun in his hand pointed in her direction.

Eleanor froze, unable to move as glass shattered on the table next to her, the gun's loud report filling the air as the SUV sped past. In those seconds after the car took the corner and disappeared, tires squealing, she didn't know if she'd been hit by the gunfire.

In the equally deafening silence that followed, she heard Willie come running up to her, heard him swear and saw his expression. She looked down expecting to see holes in her body, blood leaking out.

There was blood, but it appeared to be splatters. With a horrible dawning, she knew it wasn't hers. She turned slowly to see Phillip McNamara slumped over. The wound to his head had formed a lake of blood in the center of the table.

Chapter Thirteen

Eleanor felt numb as she sat in a corner of the restaurant with one of the officers. She'd already given her statement. Willie had cautioned her to keep it brief. She was having lunch with her boss and managing partner at the firm. She had no idea why someone would want to kill him. Or her.

She'd remained calm, spoken clearly and kept her inner turmoil from her expression. Years of practice had paid off. But every time she closed her eyes, she saw it happening again. The man wearing the black ski mask, the black SUV, the gun, a semiautomatic, also black. It all happened so fast.

That was what she'd told the officer.

Outside, through the shattered front window of the restaurant and the driving rain, she could see Willie with the police chief. She could tell just from their expressions and postures that the chief was chewing him out. It appeared that his time in Seattle had run out.

Yet, she couldn't imagine him walking away from this. Walking away from her, knowing she might still be in danger. Had those bullets been for her? Had the shooter missed and killed Phillip by accident? Or had her boss been the target all along?

Willie finished his conversation and headed for the front door of the restaurant. She tried to read his face as he approached, but he was as good at hiding his inner turmoil as she was, she realized. Their gazes met through the rain and held for a moment. He winked and pushed open the door.

A wave of relief washed over her. She had no idea what he'd told the chief, but Willie wasn't the kind of man who gave up. She felt warmth radiate through her—even as she warned herself not to get too attached to this man. Once he completed what he'd come to Seattle to do, he'd head back to Lonesome. Nothing could keep him in the big city. Certainly not a "buttoned-up" lawyer.

That thought brought the fresh reminder of Phillip slumped over the table, dead. She felt tears burn her eyes. What was going on?

Willie took off his wet jacket, slung it on the back of the booth and slid in next to her. Without a word, he put an arm around her, pulled her into his chest and began stroking her back. She'd been allowed to wash up in the restroom, but her clothing was still splattered with Phillip's blood. At first she was tense in Willie's arms, but after a moment, she felt herself let go. She breathed in his outdoor scent, her cheek warm against his shirt, his arms reassuring around her.

After a few moments, she pulled back. Being in his arms felt too good, too comfortable, too safe when she knew different. "The chief—"

"Don't worry about him."

"I'm not. I'm worried about you."

He chuckled. "I'm fine. How are you holding up?"

She nodded, swallowing. "Do you think…"

"That you were the target? I don't know. Maybe both of you were. I wounded the shooter. Hopefully that will make him easier to find."

Eleanor stared at him. "You were firing, too?" She'd heard all those shots, but she'd just assumed the man in the speeding SUV had missed her, the shots going wild. Of course Willie would have fired back. "Is that why the chief is upset with you? You don't have any authority out here."

Willie nodded. "He's threatening to put me in jail if I'm not out of town by sundown."

"What are you going to do?" She waited, heart in her throat.

"Get out of this restaurant, for starters. Come on." He stepped from the booth, pulled on his jacket and then helped her with hers before leading her to his patrol SUV parked a block away. Once they were inside, buckled up and moving, he asked, "What do you want to do now, Eleanor?"

He only called her Eleanor when he was scared, she thought.

WILLIE WOULDN'T HAVE blamed her if she was ready to catch the next plane out of Dodge until this was over. He knew the feeling.

Ellie looked over at him. He'd seen emotions wash over her face—shock, fear, sorrow and now anger. But no tears. He thought she might still be in shock. "I want to catch those sons of—" Her voice broke. "Don't try to send me away again. I'm going to see this through one way or the other."

The determination in her voice didn't surprise him. She was strong. Still, he didn't like the *one way or the other.* "Are you sure?"

She nodded, catching her lower lip in her teeth for a moment. "If you're right about someone at the police station tipping off the men who attacked you and took Vernon, then we can't trust them to stop these people."

"You're sure your boss didn't tip them off and that's why he's dead?"

Willie listened as she filled him in. He was surprised at the information she'd been able to get out of the man. The missing ring was a whole new twist. So was the wife's claim that her husband had been behind the killing of Zoey Bertrand—and instead of wanting a reconciliation, he was trying to kill Angeline, too, for the insurance money.

He'd wanted to dislike her boss, but now wondered if the man really hadn't known the case would be this dangerous for Ellie. He got the feeling that Phillip McNamara was still carrying a torch for her and had been hoping he might have a chance with her after all.

"What do we do now?" she asked.

He gave it only a moment's thought. "For starters, call Colt Brothers Investigation." He pulled out his phone. The rain had slowed to a patter that danced on the top of the patrol SUV, running like tears down the window. Outside, the day was a bruised variation of grays.

James answered. He filled him in on what had happened and the ultimatum the chief of police had given him.

"Sounds like you've worn out your welcome in Seattle."

"Does seem that way, but I can't leave yet."

"Willie, I don't like what's happening."

"Nor do I. That's why I need you to check into Lowell Carter's finances. His wife, Angeline, seems to think he knocked off his girlfriend to get back a very expensive ring he'd given her. She also believes he wants to get her, too. Something about a ten-million-dollar possibly double indemnity insurance policy on her life for accidental death?"

James let out a low whistle. "A nice cash payout, if he's short on funds."

"I need to know more about this engagement ring Carter allegedly bought Zoey that is allegedly worth a small fortune. Ellie's boss said it wasn't found on the body. I don't remember seeing anything about it in the police report. If it exists, someone has it. Could be why Vernon might have been tortured by the men who abducted him."

"Seems like a stretch," his brother said.

"That's my feeling, too, but it does add a new wrinkle."

"Am I going to have to get you out of jail?" He could hear the worry in his brother's voice. Jail was nothing compared to what James was really worried about. This could get him killed and they both knew it.

"Possibly," he said, looking over at Ellie. "If that happens, I need you to make sure attorney E.L. Shafer is safe." He smiled and winked at her. "Thanks, I knew I could count on you."

"Be careful."

"Always." He disconnected and considered her. He hated to even ask, but time was running out. "You still up to going to Ellensburg to have a talk with Zoey Bertrand's old boyfriend KY? I'd like to know more about her. Was she the type of woman who'd turn him in to the authorities? Also, we still need to get you some real clothes for the occasion."

She cocked a brow at him. "I can't wait to see what you consider *real* clothes."

Eleanor stared at the woman in the mirror. She felt like the city mouse gone country in a story her nanny used to read to her. Willie had taken her shopping, sending her into a dressing room saying he'd bring her what she needed.

"Don't you want to know my sizes?" she'd asked him.

"Trust me," he said with a grin. "Let's see if I'm as good at dressing you as you were me."

She did trust him. Now, looking in the mirror at the clothes he'd brought her to try on, she had to admit he'd been almost too good at guessing her sizes. The boot-cut jeans fit like a glove. She'd never owned a pair of cowboy boots in her life. The leather was soft, the boots surprisingly comfortable. She couldn't imagine what they'd set him back. The Western snap shirt was gray-and-white check, the gray matching her eyes, something she knew hadn't been an accident.

When she came out of the dressing room, she saw his eyes widen. He seemed at a loss for words as he gave her a thumbs-up. "But the hair..." She stood perfectly still as he moved to her and removed the scrunchie she'd used to pull her hair up into a messy bun on top of her head.

A shiver moved through her as she felt his fingers running through her hair. She had to bite her lip to keep from sighing with pleasure. The man had nice hands. He drew her long hair into a low ponytail to one side and took a step back to assess her. His smile told her everything she needed to know.

Willie tossed her a jean jacket and paid the bill. "You ready?"

As they drove over the mountain to Ellensburg, they discussed everything they'd learned and agreed that there were too many holes in the information they'd gathered. They still didn't know who'd hired Vernon or who had him now and why.

"I'm hoping KY will fill in some of those holes," Willie said. "This place we're going, it could be rough."

She smiled. "Don't worry, power suit or not, I'll be fine."

THE SHAFT TURNED out to be a metal building in an industrial area. A half dozen pickups were parked around it. Ellie had managed to find a recent photo of Kevin

Yates online. His Facebook page showed a blue-collar drinking man, most of the photos taken in bars with KY clearly overserved. From what they gleaned on his page, Zoey wasn't his first failed relationship.

Willie pushed open the door. A roar of loud voices, the smell of stale beer and the clatter of pool balls rushed out. They stepped into the dark bar, blinking until their eyes adjusted. Willie led Ellie over to a table in the corner, then went to place their orders at the bar. A skinny woman with a hoarse voice asked what he wanted. "Two beers. Whatever you have on tap." He tossed down a twenty, and she took it and headed down the bar.

He spotted a group of raucous men, KY at the center and clearly the loudest of the group. The bartender returned with his beers and his change. He passed her a ten-dollar bill and, leaning in, said, "Would you tell KY that we're over here and want to buy him a drink? Thanks." He turned, taking the two beers to the table and sitting down across from Ellie. She'd made herself comfortable, putting her boots up on an empty chair and leaning back against the wall.

He couldn't believe how different she looked in the clothing he'd gotten her. Even her attitude was different. If anything, she looked stronger, more confident, more determined than she'd been in her power suit and heels.

Willie had known she would look kick-ass in jeans and boots. She did. She'd left the two top buttons of the Western shirt undone, exposing her throat and a patch of lightly freckled skin. When he met her eyes, he had to laugh. Nothing buttoned-up about this woman tonight.

Like him, she'd spotted KY.

He watched the bartender give the man the message. KY looked in their direction. Willie raised his glass and smiled. KY glanced at him, frowning. Then the man's gaze landed on Ellie. KY took a long drink of his beer, said something to his buddies and extricated himself from his friends to saunter over.

Kicking out a chair for the man to sit down, Willie said, "This is Ellie. What are you drinking?"

KY took the chair and sat, grinning at the lawyer. "I'd take another beer." Willie signaled the bartender. The group of men KY had left were watching them closely. So was the bartender. Willie pointed to KY. She got the message.

Ellie dropped her boots to the floor and leaned toward the heavy-equipment operator. "We have some friends in common," she said to him as Willie returned from the bar with the man's beer.

"Is that right?" KY said.

Willie set the beer in front of him and took his chair again.

"You used to work at a mine in Montana, right?" she asked.

KY nodded, took a gulp of his beer and asked, "How did you know that?"

"Vernon Murphy. He told me if I was ever out this way, I should look you up."

"Spark?" KY sounded surprised by that, but not

sorry. The man gave Ellie a lecherous look. "How is it you know Spark?"

Willie decided to move things along. He leaned forward, placed his badge on the table where the rest of the bar couldn't see it, and said, "Tell us about Zoey."

KY jerked back at the sight of the badge. "What the—" He started to rise.

"We just want to ask you a few questions," Ellie said quickly, touching his arm to keep him seated. "You know Spark's in trouble, right?"

"I don't know anything about it." Maybe he didn't.

"But you used to date Zoey," Willie said.

"I didn't have anything to do with her death. Spark's the one who blew her up. Not me." So he knew that much.

"We want to know who hired him, who set him up," Ellie said, drawing KY's attention back to her. It wasn't hard. KY was clearly smitten with her, and Willie knew the feeling. "I'd think you'd want whoever did this to pay."

"Zoey and I weren't together anymore," the man said sullenly. "Why would I give a fat—"

"I know you still cared," Ellie said. "All the times you tried to see her."

"Until the bitch got a restraining order on me." KY finished the beer he'd brought over to the table and put the bottle down a little too hard.

"Still," Ellie said. "I can't imagine that you wanted her dead. But I suspect she really hurt you when she hooked up with Lowell Carter. That had to be hard to take. If it was me, I'd be furious. Good riddance to bad rubbish."

Picking up the fresh beer, KY took a gulp before putting it down. "Yeah, maybe she got what she deserved."

"Any chance you had her killed?" Willie asked.

KY swore and reached for his beer again. He'd clearly already had enough to make his face flushed and slack, his eyes slightly unfocused. "Everyone knows Spark killed her." He mumbled something unintelligible, then said, "Blasters always think they're better than the rest of us. That little sawed-off, loudmouthed Spark was way too big for his britches." He drank some of his beer. "Guess he got what he deserved, too," he said, licking the foam off his lips.

"Are you saying he's dead?"

That stopped the cocky, heavy-equipment operator. "How would I know? I just meant he's got the law after him *finally*. Everyone knew what he did on the side."

"Did his boss Lowell Carter?" Ellie asked.

KY laughed. "He didn't have a clue."

Willie jumped in. "You hire him to kill your girlfriend?"

The man shook his head. "If I wanted her dead, I would have killed her myself with my bare hands." Willie got the impression KY had given this some thought before tonight.

"Except she had that restraining order on you and this time you would have gone to jail if you got near her, let alone touched her," Willie said. The man brushed that off, as if going to jail was nothing. "You told her you'd see her dead before you'd see her with Lowell Carter." He didn't know this for a fact, but he knew KY's type.

The man shrugged. "I say a lot of things, especially when I'm mad." He snorted. "Or drunk." He took a long pull on his beer bottle. His gaze went back to Ellie. "You a cop, too?"

She shook her head. "Attorney."

"Really? I might need one after tonight." KY laughed.

Willie noticed that the man's friends over at the bar were no longer watching with concern, but they'd still be curious. Not that Willie and Ellie looked out of place in this bar. He saw several cowboy hats and some boots. He'd rodeoed here when he was young, so he knew Ellensburg.

Ellie shifted in her seat, knocking her purse to the floor. Earlier, she'd hooked the strap of the bag over the back of her chair. As it landed, she reached for it. KY lurched to the side, leaning down to help her, and practically fell out of his chair. He had to catch himself by grabbing the edge of the table. The beer glasses wobbled.

It took a few minutes for Ellie, with KY's inept help, to pick up what had fallen from her purse.

Willie sighed. He could see that if they were going to get anything out of KY, they'd better hurry. "You really didn't see a way to get rid of Zoey and Vernon and pay back Lowell Carter—all at the same time?" Willie asked after Ellie had retrieved her purse. Out of the corner of his eye, Willie saw that she was applying lipstick and taking her time doing it—and KY was watching with a drunken leer.

KY slowly dragged his gaze away from Ellie, as if confused for a moment. "That would make me awfully damned smart, wouldn't it?" Grinning, he asked, "You don't think I'm that smart, do you, *Deputy*?"

"Who then was behind it?" he asked.

KY shook his head. "You're right about one thing. If I ever get my hands on the person…" He looked up, locking eyes with Ellie. "I loved that woman. What they did to her…" He finished his beer and shoved to his feet. "Thanks for the drink." He cocked his head at Ellie. "You should come back sometime without the cowboy cop." He raised his almost empty beer bottle in salute and staggered back to his friends.

Willie took a sip of his beer, placed a tip on the table and rose. "Let's leave before he tells his friends I'm a cop and you're a lawyer."

Once in his patrol SUV, he turned to her. "You were amazing in there. I apologize for putting you in that situation."

She waved off his apology as she pulled her phone from her jean jacket pocket. "It was my choice. I knew how it would go."

"Still." He started the patrol SUV and pulled out of the parking lot. "What's your take on KY?"

"He could have done it. He knew all the players." She was scrolling on the phone in her lap. "He was also a little too proud of himself. If he did it, he's going to brag about it to someone. Truthfully, he doesn't seem smart enough to have planned it alone, though."

"Someone could have put him up to it. Paid him," Willie said, wondering what she was looking for on the phone. "If he's guilty and wasn't working alone, I'm betting he'll contact the person after our visit."

"He won't be calling anyone for a while," she said, and held up the phone in her hand. "I took his cell phone when I dropped my purse. It was hanging out of his side pocket. He didn't even realize he'd lost it."

Willie shook his head. "You really are something. You managed to get into the phone?"

"It's an old phone and he didn't have it password-protected," she said. "Probably didn't want the hassle when he was drinking. I'm not sure how much it's going to help, though. I only recognize one contact name on it." She looked over at him and grinned. "Lowell Carter."

"If I wasn't driving, I'd kiss you."

ELEANOR KNEW HE was joking, but still his words were like a beam of sunlight, warming her. It was the look in his eyes though that sent the missile of scorching heat to her center.

She dragged her gaze away to look out at the night as she reminded herself that she couldn't get too attached to this man. Once this wild ride was over, the cowboy would be galloping off into the sunset. She had no idea what she'd be doing when that happened, she realized.

Settling in for the long drive, she tried to make sense of what she was doing with this man. Her boss was dead. The memory came as a shock, one she knew she hadn't fully accepted. She couldn't even be sure that she still had a job. What surprised her was that she didn't feel that upset about the job and had conflicting emotions about her boss. McNamara had gotten her into this. Maybe he hadn't known how dangerous it was—until the shooting started. But he'd made working at the firm almost impossible after she'd rebuffed his advances.

Maybe giving her Vernon Murphy's case had been more punishment for rejecting him. Maybe everything he'd said to her at that table before the shooting had been a lie, and those bullets had been for her. Still, she hoped that she wasn't the reason he was dead.

She closed her eyes, realizing how exhausted she was after the long, emotional day. She worried they would never find out the truth. At some point, Willie would have to go home to Montana. At some point, she'd have to do what? Go back to her old life? Right now she couldn't bear the thought.

Eleanor woke to Willie's hand on her shoulder.

"Hey, Cinderella, we're back from the ball," he said.

She struggled to fully wake up, still caught in what she now knew had been a dream. She felt the dream slipping away like mist drifting across the Sound as she sat up. All she knew was that Willie had been in the dream—and she'd been naked. That was disturbing enough. "Where are we?"

Not Seattle. All she could see were pine trees and darkness, except for a lone light shining on a log house. *"Willie?"*

Chapter Fourteen

Her tone alone warned him everything was about to hit the fan. He'd made good time, driving over the speed limit from Ellensburg. He kept thinking about his earlier words. "If I wasn't driving, I'd kiss you."

He would have kissed her. He had wanted to kiss her. He'd wanted a lot more than that, he'd thought as he'd looked over at her, surprised that she'd fallen asleep.

In that moment, he'd felt such a mixture of overwhelming emotions, most of them so alien to him, that he felt lost. It terrified him that he might get this smart, ingenious, amazing woman killed and he'd changed his plans. He'd taken the first exit, gotten back on the interstate and headed to the one place he knew would be safe for her.

"We're in Lonesome, Montana."

"Wha—" She was awake now.

"Come on, I want you to meet my brother James and his wife, Lori." He started to open his door, but she grabbed his arm.

"What is going on?" she demanded, those gray eyes clouded with anger.

He sighed and looked out into the darkness before he told her the truth. "The police chief in Seattle as well as my boss here made it clear that if I wasn't back in Lonesome by tonight, I was fired and headed for jail."

That didn't seem to be the answer she'd anticipated. "You're giving up?"

Willie met her gaze and smiled. "Unfortunately, it isn't in my nature to give up, on anyone or anything I care about."

She looked toward the house. "Then why— If you think—"

He didn't let her finish as he reached for her, cupping her chin and turning her to face him. "I realized I was going to get you killed. I couldn't bear that thought even before I started caring so much about you." He watched her reaction to his words.

When she spoke, some of her anger had dissipated. "So you kidnapped me?"

"I've taken you under protective custody for the night."

Ellie snorted. "You have no legal right to do that."

"Take me to court," he said, releasing her chin to open his door.

As he started to step out, she said, "Are you prepared to remove me bodily from this vehicle?"

He stopped and turned back to grin at her. "If I have to, I promise to try not to enjoy it."

She swore and threw open her door, bounding out. "You can't keep me here."

Willie climbed out and looked across the top of the SUV at her. The fire in her eyes stirred him as much as the curve of her hips in the jeans he'd bought her. This woman was going to be the death of him, he thought.

He softened his tone. "Come meet some of my family. At least for tonight, we're both safe. We can talk about it in the morning." She looked toward the house. His brother James had come out to stand under the porch light. He saw her surprise at the resemblance between them.

"How many of you are there?"

"Just four—that I know of," he joked. "Women did love my father and people say we've all taken after him."

She harrumphed but let him lead her toward the house and the brother waiting on the porch for them. He didn't kid himself. He'd seen that flash of fury in her eyes and known that she might never forgive him for this.

That realization hurt more than he wanted to admit.

Chapter Fifteen

"You're probably going to need help getting those off." From the doorway, Willie saw Ellie sitting on the edge of the bed. He could tell from her expression that she'd already tried to remove the boots herself. She had a frustrated, angry look he recognized. E.L. Shafer wasn't a woman who enjoyed failing at anything. He suspected that was in part why she was still furious with him. He didn't have to guess what the other part was. He motioned to her boots as he closed the guest room door behind him.

"You're...impossible," she said as he approached her.

"I know." He hunkered down in front of her and pushed up her jeans. Wrapping his hands around her booted foot, he removed one boot, then the other. Setting them aside, he avoided her gaze.

She'd hidden her anger at him when she'd met James and Lori before they were shown to the guest room and his brother and wife returned to bed. Ellie had been nice and polite, and he could tell that she liked Lori, but then everyone did. James had looked worried, just as he'd sounded on the phone when Willie had called to tell him that he was bringing Ellie to Lonesome.

"Do you think that's wise?" his brother had asked.

"I can't leave her in Seattle. It's too dangerous." He heard James's question in the silence that followed. "She's been a big help with navigating this huge city and filling in gaps in the investigation." More silence. "I care about her, okay?"

"You can't keep her. You do realize that, right?"

Earlier, Lori had apologized, saying that they had only one guest room. "But there's a couch in it that Willie can take or—"

"They'll figure it out," James had said, and taken his wife's hand. "Good night. We'll see you both in the morning."

Now he could feel Ellie watching him. He slowly raised his head. Her gray eyes shimmered as if filled with a light from inside. She hadn't cried, not even a tear, after the attack in the alley or after seeing her boss killed next to her.

Willie could see so much in her face now, emotions she'd held back since they'd met, emotions she'd kept locked down. He suspected she was a woman who'd been raised to always be in control. It was as if she'd been putting on that buttoned-up lawyer veneer like she did her power suit and heels each morning for years, and now felt naked.

He reached for her, drawing her to him, half expecting her to slap him—or worse, push him away. She did neither. She fell into his arms, pressing her face against his shoulder. He felt the quake of her silent sobs, felt the dampness, felt her give up any semblance of control as she held on to him as if in a violent storm.

Pressing his face into her hair, he closed his eyes, rocking her, he, too, in a storm of his own. He more than cared for this woman and it terrified him—and at the same time, just the sight of her filled his heart to overflowing. He would catch just a hint of her scent or make her smile or hear her laugh or feel her breath on his cheek and realize that he'd never felt this alive.

Having her in his arms—even for a few minutes...

She pulled back to wipe her tears on her shirt-sleeve before she met his gaze. Their eyes locked and he couldn't catch his breath as she leaned toward him and pressed her lips to his.

As HER LIPS touched his, Willie drew back. His eyes searched hers, but for only an instant, and then his mouth was on hers. Hungrily, he kissed her with a passion that could only match her own. Her lips parted as she opened up to him, surrendering to these feelings that had been plaguing her since he'd walked into her office. With this man it would be total surrender.

Eleanor had spent her life regimented, from how she interacted with her lawyer parents to how she attacked her classes at university and law school, and finally how she took on her job at the firm. Everything had been well-ordered, because the law had its rules to follow. She'd never considered stepping off the path, breaking those rules, changing her course.

Until cowboy deputy Willie Colt burst into that disciplined life with his untamed, boundless thirst for doing the right thing—no matter the consequences. He'd torn down barriers she hadn't even known she'd constructed. He'd brought into question everything about her life and how she had lived it. Especially her love life. She'd chosen men like herself, by-the-law lawyers who didn't have a wild bone in their bodies. Men nothing like Willie Colt.

He pulled her to her feet, his hands cupping her buttock as he deepened the kiss. Her nipples ached, hard-tipped and yearning for his mouth on them as he let go of her and slowly began to unsnap her Western shirt. With the sound of each snap being released she felt a bolt of heat pierce her center. Goose bumps raced across her skin. She craved the warmth of his big warm hands, his hard body.

She'd never wanted a man like she did this cowboy. As he opened her shirt, he pulled down her bra to suck a nipple into his mouth. She moaned with pleasure as he laved the tip with his tongue before moving on to the other breast while he unhooked her bra, slipped off her shirt and cast it aside.

Needing to feel his bare skin against hers, she pulled at the snaps on his Western shirt, making them sing as they opened. She pressed into him, her full breasts soft against his warm, hard chest. Hearing his moan, her desire mounting, she worked at the rodeo buckle on his belt, then at the buttons on his jeans as he stripped off her jeans and panties with the same urgency.

Kicking off his boots and jeans, he grabbed her and practically threw her onto the bed. She felt a laugh escape her lips before his mouth covered hers again. His

hands roamed over her, touching places that sent shiv-
ers through her, intensifying everything. She thought
she'd burst even before she felt his fingers gently work
her thighs apart. Her head fell back with a cry of deca-
dent desire as he gently stroked her.

It took only his touch to take her to the zenith. She
cried out from the release only to feel it building once
again as he moved up her body, his lips making their
way to hers as he filled her, fulfilled her, taking her to
unimaginable new heights before his release.

He collapsed beside her, pulling her over into his
arms as they both fought to catch their breaths. Her
body was still alive, her skin sensitive even to the air
around them. His body, skin hot to the touch, felt like
a warm fire next to hers.

When she met his eyes, she saw her own wonder
mirrored in his. There were no words. She could feel a
cool breeze coming in the open window, bringing the
scent of pine from the remainder of the night. They
didn't have to find words for what had just happened
between them, she thought as she curled against him
and fell into the best sleep she'd had in her life.

She woke to sunlight streaming into the guest room,
almost believing that last night's lovemaking had been
nothing but a dream.

Then she turned and met Willie's blue gaze and felt
him reach for her yet again.

Chapter Sixteen

Later that morning, James looked up as Willie came into the kitchen. All it took was one glance at his older brother for James to apparently know that he hadn't slept on the couch. He shook his head and said, "I hope you know what you're doing."

Willie scoffed at that. "Did you know what you were doing when you ran into Lori again?" he asked as he took a chair across from his brother at the table.

"You always swore that you were never going to fall in love."

"Who says I'm in…love?"

James laughed. "You're a goner and you don't even realize it yet."

Willie thought about last night. "I've never met anyone like Ellie…" He couldn't put the feeling into words this morning any more than he could last night. Nor did he want to. It felt too intimate, too personal, too intense and too new.

His brother chuckled. "There is no fool like a fool in love, especially in your case."

"What's this talk of fools in love?" Lori asked as

she came into the kitchen. She looped an arm around her husband's neck and kissed his cheek before coming over to hug her brother-in-law. "Don't listen to him. I'm making pancakes and bacon. James, didn't you even offer your brother a cup of coffee?"

"We've been busy talking," her husband said.

"Don't let me stop you." Lori went behind the kitchen island and returned with a cup of coffee.

Willie thanked her and asked his brother, "What did you find out about Lowell Carter's finances?"

James seemed as glad of the change of topic as Willie. "He's facing a lot of EPA fines from the messes he left behind when he abandoned mining operations in a variety of states. A lot of his investors have pulled out, including Jonathan Asher."

"So Asher isn't involved with him anymore?"

"At least not that I could find," James said. "But his other investors probably aren't happy. Right now Cascade Extraction Corp is shut down, and from what I can tell, there isn't much if any money coming in—at least not from mining. By the way, the building outside of Lonesome wasn't the only one owned by the corporation that was torched in the past two years— and insurance collected on it."

"Maybe Angeline Carter is right about her husband trying to cash in on her life insurance policy," Willie said as Ellie came into the kitchen. He met her gaze, making her cheeks flush before she looked away. He couldn't help but think of the two of them tangled in the sheets again this morning. Nor had he ever felt like this before. It was as if he was floating. The cold shower he'd taken had done little to bring him back down to earth—a place he really needed to be right now. These newfangled feelings scared the hell out of him, and at the same time, he'd never felt happier.

Lori got her a cup of coffee, declining Ellie's offer to help with breakfast. "You just join the men. James said you've been a great help to Willie out in Seattle, so I'm sure you're interested in what James has found out."

"I'm not sure how much help I've been," Ellie said as she took her coffee over to the table. Willie could tell that she was touched by not just the hospitality but the acceptance of her being part of the investigation.

"So, how broke is Carter?" Willie asked.

"As broke as any man who made his fortune with other people's money," James said. "He won't go hungry."

"Do you think he was desperate enough to hire Vernon to torch his building, kill his fiancée and get the ring back?" Willie asked.

Before James could answer, Ellie said, "Vernon didn't get the ring. I don't think he even knew about it. He told me about his shock at seeing Zoey at the window and I believe him. He was scared. He knew he'd been set up to take the fall for her death. He'd run. He wasn't in on it."

The two men looked at her for a long moment before Willie nodded and said, "So, where's the ring?"

"Pawnshop?" James joked.

"Not if it's worth as much as Angeline Carter told her lawyer it is," Ellie said. "But she could have lied to my boss about it, although he believed her."

"Sounds like if you find the ring, you'll find your killer," his brother said.

"If the ring even exists," Ellie said, drawing both his and James's attention. "Did anyone see it on her finger?"

JAMES MADE A quick call to Zoey's sister to ask about the ring. As he disconnected, he said, "There *was* a ring. A large emerald surrounded by diamonds. Apparently, Zoey had been afraid to wear it to work, fearing she might lose it. The sister said she looked for it in Zoey's apartment, but it wasn't there. She says that her sister must have been wearing it when she died."

"If she left it at home, wouldn't the police have found it when they were investigating her murder?" Eleanor asked.

Willie nodded. "So who has it?"

As the brothers' conversation turned to the ranch and the investigation business, Eleanor went into the kitchen, determined to help Lori. "Thank you for opening up your house to us in the wee hours of the morning."

Lori smiled and touched her arm. "Our home is always open to family."

"I'm not—"

"Not yet," the woman said with a laugh. "I've seen the way my brother-in-law looks at you. He's never looked at a woman like that, not ever. In fact, he's always sworn he was never going to fall in love, saying it was more dangerous than being a deputy or a PI."

Eleanor wanted to argue that neither of them had

necessarily fallen in love. But she could no more explain this feeling than make excuses for why she'd ended up in his arms last night. She'd wanted Willie and had never wanted another man with that kind of intensity.

Lori's look softened. "I've known Willie my whole life. I've never seen him like this. I love seeing him so…happy. You have a glow about you as well," she said, smiling.

She didn't know what to say. Nor did she get the chance. Lori handed her a huge platter full of pancakes and bacon, then followed her out to the table carrying plates and silverware. The conversation changed to the antics of the wild Colt brothers in their youths.

Eleanor found herself laughing as she enjoyed the warmth in this house along with her breakfast. She listened as Lori told the story of how she and James fell in love, laughing over a sandwich she'd made him full of hot peppers.

"I ate it. Every bite," James said. "It hurt all the way down—and for days later, but it was worth it." A lovely look passed between husband and wife.

"I'm sorry you didn't get to meet our daughter, Jamie," Lori said. "My sister-in-law Bella picked her up this morning. Bella's pregnant and needed a baby fix." Lori laughed. "Did James tell you that we're expecting again? It's a boy." Her smile told it all.

Eleanor congratulated the happy couple and helped clear the table. As she and Lori filled the dishwasher, she thanked her again.

"You are welcome here anytime." She paused as if

to study Eleanor. "I hope you'll be back. I worry about how dangerous this line of work is, but I can also see that all four of the Colt brothers love trouble. They just can't stay out of it." She shrugged and reached for Eleanor's hand. "Take care of yourself and Willie. I know he'd risk his life for you."

"That's what worries me," Eleanor said.

"Just be careful with his heart," Lori said, and squeezed her hand before letting go. "Please don't break it."

"I FORGET HOW much this place grounds me," Willie told Ellie. He'd brought her outside out on the porch and into the sunshine under an azure blue, cloudless sky. The air smelled of pine and the nearby creek. Birds sang from the tree boughs. There was no sound of traffic, no honking horns, no blare of sirens. There was only the whisper of the breeze sighing high in the tops of the pines.

"I can see that," she said. "This place and your family." She felt it as well. Here, she felt safe, as if insulated from the outside world. Seattle and the trouble there seemed a million miles away.

"While I'm in town, I need to go see my boss," Willie said with a sigh. "Would you mind following me in my pickup down to the sheriff's department?" At her confused look, he said, "I'm pretty sure that I'll be turning in the patrol SUV and my badge—either because I lost Vernon and didn't come right back to Lonesome, or because the sheriff isn't going to like that I'm going back to Seattle to finish what I started.

I'll have to quit. It's possible that Sheriff Henson here tipped off whoever took Vernon." He shrugged. "I don't know whom to believe anymore."

"So you're going to need a ride," Ellie said, and cocked her head as if sensing what was coming.

He looked down at his boots for a moment, his Stetson in his hand, and said, "You know that I wish you'd stay here with my family so I know you're safe." Before she could open her mouth, he rushed on, "But if I've learned anything about you, it's that you are your own woman, with a damned good mind and good instincts. I respect that. It's up to you what you do next."

ELEANOR HAD BEEN ready to argue. For a moment she didn't know what to say. "Thank you." She stepped closer to cup his rough, stubbled jaw in her palm as she thought about their lovemaking. A quiver of desire threaded through her as she kissed him. Drawing back, she thought about what Lori had said. "I can't let you go alone. We're in this together, one way or the other."

He nodded, though she could see it was hard for him to accept. He reached into his pocket and dug out a set of keys. "You know how to drive a stick?"

"I suspect I'm about to learn," she said as she took the keys from his hand.

"I could ask my brother."

She shook her head. "I'll figure it out."

He smiled, his gaze locking with hers. "I'm sure you will," he said with a laugh. "Follow me. Not too close," he added, and grinned.

She hadn't seen anything of the area around James

and Lori's house in the pines last night. As she followed Willie in the patrol SUV with a lot of jerks and stops that required restarting the pickup, she caught glimpses of mountain peaks and clear running creeks.

The trees opened to a two-lane blacktop. Willie turned onto the highway and minutes later a town appeared. Welcome to Lonesome, the sign read. She felt as if she'd been dropped into a Western film. The town was quaint with its brick and wood structures that seemed as if they were straight off a movie set.

Willie turned into the sheriff's department parking lot. After a couple of unsuccessful tries, she did as well in his truck. By the time she turned off the pickup's engine, she felt as if she was starting to get the hang of driving a stick. It made her smile. Although she couldn't imagine driving it in the city. Or possibly ever driving one again.

The feeling that this was all a dream and that she would soon wake up left her feeling despondent. She didn't want to wake up and have never known Willie Colt.

Just the thought of their lovemaking came with both pleasure and pain. Lori seemed to think that this could last, this wild fling with Willie Colt. All she could think was, a fish and a bird could fall in love, but where would they live?

She tried not to think about the future. All she knew for sure was that Deputy Willie Colt had turned her life inside out in a matter of days. Was it any wonder that her old life felt like a blur after everything she'd been through since the cowboy had walked into her office?

She made herself think about Seattle and her job—if she still had one. She figured one of the other partners had taken over managing the firm. She had no idea where that left her. Maybe out in the cold.

Her cell phone rang. Not the burner she'd used to call Phillip, but her own. She dug it out, thinking it would be Willie, since he'd been inside for a while. Maybe he'd been arrested. Maybe he needed bail rather than a ride.

She didn't recognize the number. Was it possible that Vernon could be calling her again?

She looked toward the sheriff's department—no sign of Willie—and quickly took the call. "Hello?"

Chapter Seventeen

Sheriff Henson leaned back in his chair, his fingers entwined across his large extended belly, as he considered Willie. From the expression on the older man's face, this was going to get uglier.

"I knew you weren't going to work out," Henson said. "I've watched you Colt boys behaving like a pack of wolves for years." He shook his head. "But the mayor, bless her tender soul, asked me personally to give you a chance."

"I didn't realize Beth had done that," Willie said, touched. Mayor Elizabeth Conrad had gone to school with Willie's father. The two had been friends and maybe more. "I'll have to thank her."

Henson scoffed. "A little late for that, since I can't have a man on the force who doesn't follow orders."

"I came back as soon as I could."

The sheriff side-eyed him. "You caused a pack of trouble out there. I got a call from the police chief—"

"The bottom line is that they aren't doing anything to find Vernon Murphy."

"I'm sure it isn't a top priority for them," Henson

said. "They have an entire city to keep safe. One two-bit arsonist probably isn't even on their radar."

"He killed a woman."

"Which might get him second-degree murder if he didn't know she was in the building. Face it, you blew this, Deputy Colt. It's on your head."

"That's why I have to go back. I have to—"

"You aren't going anywhere," the sheriff cut in.

"—find these people and bring them to justice," Willie continued, speaking over his boss.

Henson rocked forward in his chair, propelling himself to his feet. "Did you hear anything I said? Your job is hanging by a thread. I wanted to fire you, but the mayor…" He shook his head. "But if you go back to Seattle, you're out."

Willie nodded and rose from where he'd been ordered to sit. He pulled out his badge and laid it on the sheriff's desk. Then he removed his service revolver and put it beside the badge. "Guess I'd better quit then."

He told himself that he'd only taken this job because he'd thought he could find out more about his father's death from inside the sheriff's department. He'd never expected that he would like the job or that it would suit him, he thought as he removed his canvas jacket with the sheriff's department's insignia on it. He tossed the jacket on the chair he'd been sitting in.

"I didn't want it to be this way," Willie said, realizing how true that was. "But I have to see this through."

"You're just going to get yourself thrown in jail or killed," the sheriff called after him as Willie walked to the door. "Those Seattle cops aren't going to put up with your lone rider cowboy antics."

"I NEED TO see you," Angeline Carter said without pre-amble. Eleanor had hoped it was Vernon. She realized how foolish that hope had been as the woman rushed on. "I called the office. They gave me your number. I can't believe what happened to Phillip. I don't know what to do." The woman's voice broke. "I'm terrified I'm next."

"Where are you?"

"At the Vashon Island house."

"Where is your husband?"

"I don't know." She began to cry. "Why would he kill my attorney?"

"We don't know that your husband—"

"I think he's already made several attempts to kill me. Two so-called accidents in my car. I swear both times, the brakes didn't work right. And now Lowell is acting so strangely. I think he's having a breakdown. I called the police, but they said they can't do anything until he commits a crime. To which I said, 'What about shooting Phillip?'"

Eleanor saw Willie come out of the sheriff's department. She noticed right away that he wasn't wearing his deputy jacket—nor his department-issued weapon. "Why would your husband want to shoot your attorney?"

"He accused me of having an affair with Phillip, of the two of us trying to steal his money, destroying his reputation… It's all so upsetting. He keeps talking about the ring he gave to his girlfriend like he thought I had it."

"Do you have it?"

Angeline let out a bark of a laugh. "How would I have it?"

Eleanor could think of several possibilities. "Why is it so important to him to get it back?"

"Because it's worth so much, according to him."

"Wasn't it insured?" she asked. "If all he cares about is the money..."

"I hadn't thought of that. He must not have insured it before he gave it to the woman. It isn't like it has any *sentimental value*." Bitterness tinged her words. "What a fool. Giving a bauble like that to someone so irresponsible? She probably lost it. Or sold it."

"Why would you say that?" Eleanor asked as she slid over to let Willie climb behind the wheel of his pickup.

"The police said that the ring wasn't found on the woman's body."

"Perhaps whoever bound her and left her in that building took the ring. In that case, whoever hired Vernon to kill her has it." Willie raised a brow as Eleanor said into the phone, "If that were the case, Mrs. Carter, it stands to reason that if your husband was that person, then he wouldn't be asking you about the ring."

Angeline sighed. "Phillip always said you were scary smart," she commented with a note of respect. "But I told you. Lowell's not in his right mind." She let out a sob. "He said he wanted to try to make our marriage work and I believed him. I forgave him and now..."

"Have you considered getting a restraining order, Mrs. Carter?"

"Please, call me Angeline. Mrs. Carter reminds me of Lowell's mother. Bless her soul." She blew her nose, sniffling for a moment. "I can't keep kidding myself. I need to go ahead with the divorce as soon as possible. With Phillip gone…"

"I'll find out who'll be taking your case," Eleanor said.

"That's why I'm calling. He gave me you."

The woman's words stopped her cold. "Who gave you me, Angeline?"

"Phillip. He told me that if anything happened to him, you were to take over. He always said that you were the best attorney at the firm. He didn't mention me to you?"

WILLIE LISTENED AS Ellie promised to meet Angeline Carter first thing in the morning at her office. "What was that about?" he asked after she disconnected.

"Phillip McNamara apparently wanted me to handle her divorce case—if anything happened to him."

"Apparently he *did* know how dangerous it was," Willie said. Ellie didn't respond. He saw that she didn't want to argue the point, probably because she didn't want to take McNamara's side. But he could tell that she felt guilty, as if she were responsible for getting him killed. "Don't blame yourself for what happened to him."

She swallowed as she glanced over at him. "You know I feel guilty?"

He turned to grin at her. Of course he did. In a matter of days, he'd gotten so close to E.L. Shafer that he felt he knew her better than she knew herself. Yet, he wanted to know more. He wanted to know everything about her. The woman intrigued the hell out of him and that scared him.

It was now more than keeping her safe. He couldn't bear the thought of leaving Seattle. Leaving Ellie. But he didn't see how this could end any other way.

Ellie met his gaze, but quickly looked away as if she'd glimpsed the emotional battle going on under the grin. "Angeline feels she needs to get her divorce immediately," she said. "She thinks Lowell is having a breakdown and she's terrified and doesn't know where he is. She seems to think that her husband is behind Phillip's shooting—and alleged attempts on her life—as well as hiring Vernon to kill his girlfriend."

He shook his head. "I'm sorry, but why would your boss want you to have Mrs. Carter's case? Was he that desperate to get you back to work? Or did he have reason to believe that someone might try to kill him?"

"I don't know. It's not unusual for a partner to choose an attorney as backup." He grunted in response. "Do I need to ask how it went with the sheriff?"

"Nope." Willie studied her as he said, "I'm going back to Seattle as a civilian. My badge wasn't worth anything out there anyway." He reached under the seat, pulled out a small bundle and unwrapped the weapon inside. He put it in the holster on his hip and took out a box of shells. "Are you serious about representing Angeline Carter, Ellie?" he asked.

"You said you wanted to talk to her. I think she knows more than she's telling, but I also believe that she's scared and maybe with good reason. She's convinced she needs the divorce pushed through because Lowell's trying to kill her before it's granted. I need to go back as her attorney and represent her."

He nodded. "What if representing her is what got your boss killed?"

She turned to lock eyes with him. "We both want this over, right?"

Was that what she wanted? "Not if you're dead."

"For some reason Phillip wanted me to handle this," she said. "It's crossed my mind that Angeline might actually know for a fact that her husband is behind all of this and told her attorney. She might even have evidence. Client-attorney privilege, Phillip couldn't tell me or the police. But if it's in her file I might be able to talk her into going to the police with what she knows—and providing any evidence she might have. I now have access to those files."

Maybe that was Phillip's reasoning, Willie thought. But wouldn't he have tried to persuade Angeline Carter to go to the police himself? Maybe he had and that was why he was dead.

"I don't like it," he said. "Like you said, whatever Angeline might tell you is covered by attorney-client confidentiality. What if she tells you something that puts you in even more danger?"

"We need answers," she said, determination in her voice. "Angeline is scared, but if she has those answers…" He could see that tough-as-nails lawyer he'd first met. "I need to do this. If Angeline has evidence that could put Lowell away, I need to convince her to turn it over to the police."

There was no doubt that Ellie could be persuasive. But this could put her in the killer's crosshairs. If she hadn't already been.

Willie started the pickup. He knew better than to try to talk her out of it. He told himself that he would just have to find Lowell quickly. He had a feeling that Jonathan Asher might know where he was. If not him, then Alex Mattson. There was a connection there. He just had to find out what it was and use it to his advantage.

His hope was that he might get some answers before the day was over. Ellie would be meeting Angeline in the morning, so he had time.

IT WAS LATE afternoon by the time they reached Seattle. Ellie had him take her to her apartment. Willie had been quiet most of the trip home. She'd been lost in her own thoughts as well. It felt as if they'd been spinning their wheels, getting nowhere. Vernon was probably dead. Phillip certainly was, and Eleanor couldn't help thinking that she might have been as well, if not for Willie.

"I know you don't like me going back to my apartment, or my office to meet with Angeline Carter tomorrow, but I can't keep hiding," she said as she opened her apartment door and they walked inside.

"Is that what we've been doing?"

She turned to look at him. "You know what I mean."

His expression softened. "I know this has been hard for you, but I can't say I'm sorry we met."

She stepped to him and kissed him, then pulled back to look into his eyes. "I'm not sorry, either." Didn't he realize how badly she wanted the danger part of this over? She didn't know what happened afterward, but she couldn't keep living like this, not knowing if she was going to live or die, waiting for it to happen.

It wasn't just the living in limbo, her life out of her control, and everything completely out of her comfort zone. It was the fear that this cowboy was going to get himself killed. Not that she didn't know that once they found the answers, he would be gone back to Montana.

She had to do something to take back the reins of her life, and being a lawyer was something she did well. Working with the law made her feel safe. She needed the rules and regulations—unlike Willie. Mostly she needed her job to fill in the huge hole that this cowboy was going to leave in her life. Just the thought of never seeing him again after this…

He pulled her to him, kissing her with a passion that made her knees weak with longing. As he drew back, he nodded as if he could see her inner turmoil in her eyes. "I need your promise that you won't step a foot out of this apartment until I come back." His tone brooked no discussion, so she nodded, even though she wondered where he was going. Earlier at the gas station, she'd heard him making a series of calls, leaving messages.

At her high-rise apartment overlooking the city, he quickly checked every room. The apartment looked exactly as she'd left it. She couldn't imagine that any-one had been able to get past the twenty-four-hour se-curity downstairs. At least, no one had signed in since she'd been gone.

Eleanor watched Willie check for listening devices in her lamps. Under her kitchen stove hood, in her bathroom. She also saw him taking in the view in the expensive apartment as if comparing how differently they lived. She knew he'd lived on the road, sleeping in the camper part of his horse trailer at some rodeo fairgrounds.

She didn't need to be reminded of how dissimilar their backgrounds were. If it wasn't for Vernon Mur-phy, they would have never met. So, why had they? she wondered as she headed for her bedroom, needing to get a hot shower and change of clothes. Was she wish-ing that he would join her in the shower? Doubtful, since he seemed anxious to leave.

She'd just sat down on the edge of the bed to take off her boots when Willie appeared in the doorway.

"Want some help with the boots?" he asked as he moved to her. He knelt down and slipped them off. She knew she could have managed by herself since the leather had loosened up, but she didn't mind the feel of his hands or these few minutes with him.

When he looked up, she saw desire fire his blue eyes. He ran a hand up her leg inside her jeans, along her calf. She felt the aching need of her own desire for this man. His expression looked pained as his cell rang. He let out a curse and rose to his feet.

She watched him walk away, wanting to call him

back, suddenly afraid she might not ever see him again as she heard him say, "I'm on my way."

WILLIE TURNED TO see Ellie still sitting on the side of the bed. It took all his inner strength not to go to her, take her in his arms and make love, since common sense told him it could be the last time. The thought shook him to his core. He knew how dangerous meeting Lowell could be.

But it was Ellie he worried about. He knew he couldn't wrap her in cotton to keep her safe. But he wanted badly to, until this was all over. All his instincts told him that Lowell Carter was the key, and right now, he was in trouble.

He walked back toward her, stopping in the bedroom doorway. He thought about telling her who'd called and where he was going. But he could see that she was already worried. "I don't like leaving you here alone."

She cleared her voice and seemed to push the worry from her expression. "I will be fine. Call me as soon as you can, though."

"I had a gun in my glove box. I put it in your purse." He saw her glance toward her purse, which she'd dropped on the table in the corner of the bedroom. "It's a point-and-shoot handgun. All you have to do is pull the trigger." He could tell by her expression that she didn't believe she could do that. He hoped she was wrong—should she need to fire it.

"Eleanor, I…" He realized he was going to tell her that he loved her. It was on the tip of his tongue. This woman had stolen his heart. But for so many reasons, he couldn't say the words. Not now. Maybe not ever. "Be safe."

He hated leaving her. But what he'd heard in Lowell Carter's voice was that he was finally going to hear the truth.

On the way down in the elevator, he replayed the phone call in his head, listening to the man's words as well as what Lowell hadn't been saying.

"I need to talk to you," Lowell said, fear punctuating his hurried words.

"I'm listening."

"Not over the phone. You have to meet me."

He thought he'd heard a foghorn in the distance. "Why would I do that?"

"I know who killed Zoey." The man's voice broke. He rattled off an address. "You're the only person I can trust. Please. Hurry. You're my last hope."

Willie walked across the lobby and stepped out onto the dark street. He felt mist on the breeze as he hurried to his pickup. The smell of the Sound and the scents of this city were starting to feel achingly familiar because they reminded him of Ellie.

He pushed that thought away as he climbed into his truck, punched in the address on his phone and drove toward the spot Lowell Carter had said to meet him—in the warehouse district along the wharf. He kept thinking about the man's tone of voice on the phone. Anxious and strained, as if someone was holding a gun to his head.

Chapter Eighteen

Willie parked behind one of the warehouses and waited for his eyes to adjust to the dark. A foghorn sounded in the distance.

Outside the pickup cab, nothing moved in the still darkness between the warehouses. He opened his door and breathed in the dense, wet air smelling of fish and water. He was already armed with a handgun, but he wasn't taking any chances. He pulled the shotgun from behind the seat. It was loaded, since an empty gun was worthless in an emergency. He dug out the box of shells and put another four in his pocket.

He had no idea what he was walking into. That Lowell was in trouble, he'd suspected long before the phone call. The man had sounded scared. He was either hiding out or they already had him and were drawing Willie into a trap.

Quietly, he closed the pickup door. They would have heard him drive up, as noisy as the old truck was. He needed to buy a new one, but like a lot of rodeo cowboys, he had his superstitions. This pickup had gotten him to many a rodeo where he'd done well. To change trucks had seemed like a bad idea.

He hoped the pickup's luck held tonight as he cradled the loaded shotgun and moved around the warehouse toward the single light over the door of an adjacent building, where Lowell said he would be waiting.

Willie tried the door, not surprised to find it unlocked. He turned the handle and it creaked open just enough that he could see the huge empty space dimly lit. Why would Lowell want to meet here?

He shifted the shotgun to his right hand and pushed the door farther open. Empty. But beyond the vast space, he could see what appeared to be an office on the second floor. The light was on behind the shuttered windows.

Letting the door close behind him, he kept his eye on the office as he crossed the expanse, his footfalls the only sound in the cavernous space. He stopped at the bottom of the stairs and listened. No sound coming from the office that he could hear. Was Lowell alone? Willie didn't see anyone moving up there.

He glanced around, but there was little place for anyone to hide. He started up the stairs, his boots ringing on each metal step. All his instincts were on alert, all of them telling him this was a bad idea.

Sheriff Henson had called him a lone rider cowboy. It was true, but only because there was no one else he could call. He didn't trust the cops, nor did he trust Lowell's associates. Ellie was the only one he trusted, and she was home safe. There was no way he would have brought her out here, because all his instincts told him he was walking into a trap.

He was almost to the top of the stairs. He couldn't see into the office, but he could hear a noise inside like someone moving around. Swearing under his breath, he reached for the door handle, telling himself the only way it would be wired with explosives was if Vernon Murphy was in on all of this.

ELEANOR HAD BEEN lost in thought, unable to stop thinking about the call Willie had gotten—and the gun he said was in her purse. Where was he going? Who was he meeting? He hadn't told her because he hadn't wanted her to worry.

She scoffed at that. It was dangerous, that much she knew instinctively. She'd seen the way he looked at her before he left. For a moment, she'd thought he was going to say… She swallowed, her throat suddenly dry. Did he love her? Was that what he was going to say? Or was he going to say goodbye?

Her heart beat faster. Did he fear he wouldn't be coming back? She pushed off the bed, unable to accept the thought that something would happen to him and he wouldn't be coming through that door ever again.

She looked around the apartment, realizing she would be next. Willie thought so. It was why he'd gone out tonight, to try to end this. She moved quickly to her purse, opened it and lifted out the gun, surprised by how heavy it was. She'd never fired a weapon. Her parents refused to have a gun in the house. They were civilized people who used the law to fight their battles.

They would have been horrified that she had a loaded weapon in her apartment.

She quickly put the gun back in her purse, shuddering as she remembered the loud report of the gunshots outside the café—and the damage the bullets had done to Phillip. She told herself that she would never be able to pull the trigger, as her phone rang.

Eleanor snatched it up, thinking it was Willie. "Tell me you're all right," she said without preamble.

"Of course I'm not all right," snapped the female voice.

"Mrs. Carter." She couldn't help the slight groan in her voice. She should have checked caller ID, but she'd been so sure, so hopeful, that it was Willie. If she had known it was Angeline Carter, she wouldn't have answered it.

"I thought you were someone else." Eleanor cleared her voice, trying to push down her disappointment and growing fear for Willie. "Has something happened?"

"I need to talk to you tonight," the woman said. "This can't wait until morning. I'm in Seattle. I can swing by your apartment and pick you up. Say twenty minutes?"

"No." Eleanor tamped down her frustration with the woman. "I'm sorry. I'll see you in the morning at my office, but not tonight. I'm…busy."

"My life is in danger," Angeline Carter snapped.

So is mine, Eleanor thought. "Go to a hotel. You'll be safe there. I'll see you first thing in the morning." She disconnected and, taking the phone, went into the bathroom to draw a bath. It was the only thing that calmed her. *Except for Willie Colt*, she thought as nerves made her restless. *Be safe. Come back to me.*

SWEATING EVEN IN the cold of the warehouse, Willie held his breath and turned the knob. It took a moment for him to realize that no explosives had gone off. But the door refused to open any further. He pushed with his shoulder, inching it open until he saw the body on the floor.

Lowell Carter lay sprawled, his feet against the door, his ankles wrapped in duct tape, his wrists bound behind him. A wide strip of tape covered his mouth. The moment he saw Willie, he began moaning loudly as he tried to talk through the tape. But it was what Willie saw duct-taped to the man's chest that chilled him to his bones. Explosives!

Willie hurriedly reached down and tore the tape from the man's mouth and was reaching for his pocketknife to cut the explosives free, when Lowell cried, "There isn't time. This whole place is about to go up. Run!"

He looked from the man's terrified eyes to the bright red glow of the timer ticking off the seconds left and did the only thing he could. He turned, falling down the stairs as he ran. He had just reached the ground floor and was running for the outside door when the first explosion boomed behind him. A wall of heat hit him in the back, the force knocking him to his knees.

He knew at once that there were more explosions coming. Scrambling to his feet, he sprinted to the door, threw it open and lunged out into the darkness. If he could get to the other side of the adjacent warehouse next to the water...

The world behind him exploded in a fiery ball, the blast knocking him off the pier. He hit the water hard, the air forced from his lungs as he went under, the dark water dragging him deeper and deeper below the surface.

Chapter Nineteen

After a long bath that hadn't helped calm or relieve her worry, Eleanor dressed, made herself a cup of coffee and began to pace the floor. Willie had promised that he would call. He hadn't. She checked the time again. He'd been gone almost two hours. Shouldn't she have heard something by now?

She made the decision. If she didn't hear from him soon, she was calling the police. She didn't know what else to do, because she couldn't shake the feeling that he was in trouble. She checked the time again and was reaching for the phone to make the call when there was a knock at her door.

Willie. That was why he hadn't called. He had been on his way. Her heart soared. She rushed toward the door, but then stopped a few feet short, frowning. She had twenty-four-hour security downstairs. There was only one way the person could have been let in. Unless the guard had recognized Willie from before…

There was another knock. She moved to the door, looked through the peephole and felt a start. A cop in uniform was standing outside her door. He knocked again.

"Who is it?" she called, her voice cracking. Willie didn't trust the police and yet she'd been ready to call them. Only because she hadn't known whom else to call. His brothers were miles away. Now there was a cop at her door?

"I'm here about Willie Colt," he called through the door. "I'm afraid he's been in an accident." Her heart leaped to her throat. She'd known something was wrong. She'd felt it. "He gave me your address and asked me to—"

She threw the door open. "Is he all right?"

The cop was about her age, short dark hair, anxious brown eyes. "He's in the hospital. He asked me to come get you."

If Willie sent him to get her, it had to be serious. "What happened?"

"Why don't I tell you on the way. We should hurry," the officer said. "My patrol car is right outside."

"Let me grab my coat." She stepped back in, leaving the door open, and got her purse and coat. Hurrying out, she closed and locked the door. Her heart thundered in her chest, a silent prayer on her lips. Willie had to make it. There was so much unsaid between them—at least on her part.

The cop led her down the hall and into the elevator. He pressed the button once, then twice. Impatient. Were Willie's injuries that serious that every minute mattered? Her eyes filled with tears. She hastily brushed them away. She had to be strong. For Willie.

The elevator began to move. She leaned against the wall, closing her eyes as she prayed even harder. She could hear the officer moving around restlessly. She opened her eyes and noticed something she hadn't before.

He wasn't wearing his name tag on his uniform.

WILLIE COULDN'T BREATHE. His eyes flew open to cold, wet darkness. He was drowning. Again. Only this time, none of his brothers were here to pull him to the surface, to save him. He felt disoriented, his body aching. But the real pain was realizing he might never see Ellie again.

He looked up, seeing light, and frantically began to swim toward the surface. His chest ached for just one more breath, his heart ached for just one more day. As he burst through the surface, he gasped for air, lungs screaming, heart thundering in his chest. He had to get to Ellie.

As he swam to the edge of the dock, he hauled himself up onto it, ignoring the pain. He tried to make sense of everything that had happened since he'd arrived in Seattle. The sky was black with smoke, the warehouse smoldering in ruin. He could hear sirens in the distance as he spotted his shotgun where he'd dropped it before being thrown into the water.

He picked it up and staggered to his pickup parked a few warehouse buildings away. His only thought was Ellie. Pulling out his phone, he shook off the water and tried it. No dice. Anger and frustration surged through him, blurring the pain in his body as he climbed in and started the engine. He'd been set up from the moment he'd come to Seattle, and it was starting to really tick him off. He tried to put the pieces together, his mind fuzzy except for the obvious.

That explosion back there in the warehouse had Spark's name all over it, which meant the man had fooled him—and no doubt Lowell, too. But Willie couldn't believe that Vernon was acting on his own. He remembered the small, scared man he'd picked up at the police department. It hadn't been an act. He'd known someone would be coming for him, someone who terrified him. So, who was pulling the strings?

Willie had a bad feeling as he sped toward downtown. Ellie had been in danger from the get-go. He told himself that she was too smart to leave her apartment. But that didn't mean that whoever was behind this wouldn't figure out a way to get to her.

He'd put the gun in her purse, but would she use it? Just the thought of her in trouble brought pain more excruciating than being blasted into Puget Sound and almost drowning. He'd endured physical pain many times before. It had come with riding bulls in the rodeo.

But this pain in his heart? He didn't think he could stand it. This was why he'd sworn to never fall in love.

Ahead, he spotted her apartment building rising up into the dark sky as it began to rain.

HEART ALREADY POUNDING, Eleanor had a sick feeling in her stomach as she asked, "Officer...? I'm sorry, I didn't catch your name."

"Guess I forgot to put my name tag on before my

shift," he said, reaching up and touching the spot where it normally would be. "My wife wasn't home when I left. She's the one who makes sure I'm presentable. I keep telling her I'm an adult and I don't need her help." His laugh sounded more nervous than humorous. "She'll never let me live this down."

Eleanor had dealt with all kinds of clients. Some lied better than others. The liars often talked too much, filling the silence with any word that came to mind.

The elevator reached the ground floor and the cop stepped off, holding the door open with his arm as he waited for her to exit.

Eleanor had no choice. If she refused to get out, he would get back in. The close confines of the elevator were the last place she wanted to be with this man even as she told herself she was wrong about him. He wasn't who she suspected he was. He wasn't lying.

She stepped out and let the door close behind her, but she didn't head for the doors out of the building. The lobby was empty at this time of the night. A guard should have been behind the security desk. He wasn't. That alone should have warned her since the guard would have had to have let the cop in.

At the windows facing the street, darkness pressed against the rain-streaked glass. She could feel the weight of the gun in her purse. Except she knew she couldn't get to it fast enough—even if she could shoot an officer of the law.

"You still haven't told me your name," she said, meeting his gaze, and saw that his hand was already resting on the weapon holstered at his hip. She knew she could run, just as she knew he would catch her before she reached the front door.

"I'm Officer Mattson. We need to get moving, Ms. Shafer," he said. "We're wasting valuable time."

Alex Mattson, the cop Vernon had confided in and regretted doing so. Willie was convinced the cop was neck-deep in all this. Eleanor had no reason to doubt it. Out of the corner of her eye she saw him furtively unsnap his holster as he palmed the gun's grip at his hip.

Eleanor swallowed, her throat dry, her body feeling weak with fear. Even if she tried to run, she didn't think her legs would hold her. She'd been lured from her apartment by a man who wasn't taking her to Willie. Once he had her in his patrol car, who knew where he'd take her. Somewhere to kill her.

She started to turn toward the stairs that led down to the parking garage, willing her body to take flight. She could feel the adrenaline raging through her veins even before he drew his gun. She got only a few steps before he grabbed her arm, spinning her back into him. She felt the hard, cold barrel pressed against her side.

"We are going to walk outside to my patrol car. Please don't make this more difficult than it has to be." He didn't sound like a cold-blooded killer. She got the feeling he didn't want to do this. But she knew he would. He was afraid of whoever had sent him here.

"Willie Colt isn't waiting for me at the hospital, is he. Was he even in an accident?" she asked, surprised by the calm in her voice as he forced her toward the front door. She could see his cop car parked at an angle in the oval drive outside, where he said it would be.

"We're just going to ride down to the station. My boss needs to talk to you about Vernon Murphy. He has some questions and he knew you wouldn't come in unless forced."

"You aren't a good liar, Alex. I know about your involvement with Jonathan Asher and Lowell Carter." She felt him stumble a little in surprise. "I also know that Vernon Murphy confided in you while in jail, waiting to be extradited. He actually thought he could trust you. It must have been the uniform that fooled him."

"You don't know anything about me," he snapped. "You think I like this? I didn't want anything to do with any of this." He pushed open the door and they stumbled out onto the sidewalk and into the falling rain. She turned her face up to the raindrops as she rested her hand on her shoulder bag at her side. Once he had her in the patrol car she was as good as dead. She slowly began to open the zipper until she could get her hand inside to the gun.

"I know you invested in Lowell Carter's mining corporation and that it's in trouble," she said, walking as slowly as possible, as if unsteady on her feet.

"I put my life savings in it." She could hear the anger in the cop's voice. "Now I'm going to lose everything unless…"

Unless? The word hung in the air as he half dragged her by her arm toward the patrol car. His fingers bit into her flesh, the barrel of the gun still pressed against her side.

"Unless you do something for them." He'd made a deal with the devil. "Let me guess. You have to kill me." Her voice broke as she asked, "Did you also have to kill Willie?"

"No, Vernon—" He caught himself. "Just shut up, okay? I don't have a choice."

We all have a choice, she thought. But felt a wave of defeat wash over her. For a moment, she just wanted to give up. She'd been trying to stall, to keep the inevitable from happening, but if Willie was dead... She shuddered at the thought, knowing how Vernon took care of his end of things.

A sob rose in her throat as the pain seized her heart in a death grip. Grief flooded her, followed by rip-roaring rage. Mattson was a fool if he thought she'd just give up. She was going to fight to the death—just as she knew Willie Colt had done.

She spun into him so abruptly that she caught him off guard. The move broke his hold on her arm. He stumbled and she went for his gun. They wrestled for a moment, before his strength and training won out. He swore, wrenching the gun away, and shoved her toward the patrol car—no longer holding on to her.

But she could see his gun trained on her as she pushed her hand into her purse and wrapped it around the grip of the gun Willie had given her. She was going to have to shoot him, she thought as she took a step back and collided with the side of the patrol car. The cop was moving toward her, his weapon aimed at her heart. Her hand was shaking as she pulled the gun.

The roar of an engine made them both turn toward the sound as a pickup came barreling around the corner and headed right for them. She pulled the trigger.

Chapter Twenty

Willie felt his heart drop at the sight of the cop, the police car—and Ellie backed up against it in front of her apartment house.

He'd never gotten a good look at Officer Alex Mattson, but he knew that was who this had to be as the cop spun in his direction—his service revolver in his hand. Willie had his foot crushing the gas pedal to the floor, the old pickup engine a howl in his ears. He saw the cop raise his weapon—and fire.

The windshield shattered as Mattson's first bullet embedded into the passenger seat. Willie kept his foot to the metal. He saw the cop jerk, saw the gun in Ellie's hand as he closed the distance between them. The cop's second shot caught him in the shoulder, making him jerk the wheel. The pickup careened off to the right, clipping the cars parked there as he swung into the oval in front of the condo building. He struggled to hang on to the wheel, to keep from losing control, and was forced to let up on the gas.

He was only yards from Mattson when the cop started to fire point-blank at him. That was when Willie saw Ellie fire the gun again. Mattson seemed to scream in pain as the bullet hit him. He stumbled but didn't fall. For a moment he lowered his weapon, but then he spun around to turn the gun on Ellie.

Willie rammed the pickup into Mattson, heard the crunch of metal and bones and the thud of the cop's body as the truck rolled over him.

Then Willie was standing up on the brakes as the pickup skidded toward Ellie, whose eyes were wide as a deer's caught in headlights.

ELEANOR KNEW SHE was in shock. She stared at the steam roiling out from under the hood of the pickup just inches from her. She'd seen Mattson go down, but now there was no sign of him. Through the pouring rain, she couldn't make out Willie behind the wheel through what little remained of the windshield.

Eleanor felt as if she was in a fog, drifting above the scene. She heard the driver's-side door open with a groan. Willie fell out, caught himself and lurched toward her. She stared in horror. He'd been shot at least once, the front of his shirt soaked with blood.

"You're going to be fine. Everything is going to be fine," he said, his voice rough with emotion as he moved to her. She still had the gun gripped in her hand, her limbs shaking. He stepped to her and gently pried her fingers from the weapon. "Everything is all right now."

He staggered. His bloody hand grabbed the side of the police car for support but then slipped, and he slid to the concrete.

Feeling as if she was watching herself from a distance, she dropped beside Willie, pulled out her phone and called 911. Her movements robot-like, she did everything by rote, as if watching from somewhere else, while she pressed her coat to his wound to staunch the bleeding.

She heard herself saying, "You're going to be fine. Everything is going to be fine." They were his words, meaningless words. She heard the wail of sirens, the scream of an ambulance as it grew closer and closer.

It wasn't until she met his blue eyes as Willie was loaded into the back of the ambulance that she began to cry. Standing in the rain, she listened to the sound of the siren die away.

"Going to need to know what happened here," a police officer said, touching her arm to draw her attention. "Miss?"

She brushed at the tears mixing with the rain. "E.L. Shafer," she said. "I'm an attorney here in Seattle."

WILLIE WOKE IN a hospital with a sense of déjà vu. He blinked, and for a moment thought he'd dreamed everything that had happened since driving out to Seattle to pick up Vernon Murphy. But as his eyes focused, he saw his brothers rise from where they'd been waiting in the shadows. One after another they came to his bedside.

He heard James pick up the phone and ask that someone let the doctor know that Willie Colt had regained consciousness after his surgery.

His mouth felt dry as dust. "Surgery?"

"You took a bullet, man," Davy said. "You don't remember?"

"Ellie?" It came out a whisper. Tommy got him a drink of water. He looked from one to the next, his fear growing. He didn't think she'd been hit, but he couldn't remember much. He tried again. "Ellie?" he asked, his heart in his throat.

"She's fine," James said as Willie tried to rise. "Take it easy. You'll see her soon. The cops had her for a long time, but she was released. Apparently, she knew a good lawyer. She didn't want to leave you, but we sent her home to change."

He remembered the rain and blood. Hers? Or just his? He remembered that dead look in her eyes as he'd pried the gun from her hand. He knew the pain in his chest had nothing to do with a gunshot. He'd dragged her into this. He would never forgive himself. Maybe if he'd never gone to her office…

"Speaking of cops, they're anxious to talk to you," James said. "They've been waiting out in the hall for you to wake up." As if seeing that Willie wasn't ready, he added, "They can wait a little longer."

He nodded, not surprised that the cops wanted to see him. The only person he wanted to see was Ellie. After what she'd been through, he had to know that she was all right. He thought about her returning to her apartment alone with Vernon still out there.

Willie tried to sit up again. "Ellie. Vernon is still—"

Tommy shook his head. "Vernon's no longer a threat. They found a second body in the debris at the destroyed warehouse. The body is believed to be Vernon's. He'd apparently been trying to get out of the building, but either had gotten trapped or miscalculated. Either way, he's gone."

Willie lay back. Vernon was dead? Lowell was dead. Was it possible that this nightmare was really over? That Ellie had no one to fear?

The hospital room door opened, and the doctor came in to shoo his brothers out. After checking Willie over, he said, "Are you up to talking to the police? They're very anxious to speak to you."

He nodded and the doctor sent them in. Chief Landry strutted in along with a younger cop, both looking like they wanted to cuff him and haul him off to jail. Willie had expected they would once he left the hospital.

"You're a dangerous man," the chief said in his gravelly voice. "Thanks to you we've been cleaning up bodies all day. Not only did you have no jurisdiction out here, but also you aren't even a deputy in Montana anymore. You're in a hell of a lot of trouble, cowboy."

"Do you want to hear what happened or did you just come in here to chew my ass?" Willie asked.

The chief puffed up for a moment before he signaled for the cop with him to make a video recording. Willie started at the beginning, making sure that his suspicions about the police department were in his statement even though the chief kept interrupting him.

He finished with being lured to the warehouse, finding Lowell Carter trapped there with explosives strapped to him and the timer about to go off.

"You somehow managed to get away," the chief said suspiciously. "How do you explain that?"

"I move fast when I have to," Willie said. "I knew I had to get to Ellie. I figured if I was set up, she probably was, too. If Lowell Carter wasn't behind this, then who did that leave? Vernon, Jonathan Asher, Alex Mattson. I knew one of them would try to get to Ellie."

"Vernon's dead. So is Mattson. You aren't suggesting that Jonathan Asher had anything to do with this?" Landry demanded.

"I know that Jonathan Asher had invested in Lowell Carter's mining company and was somehow involved with your officer Alex Mattson. Someone was giving Vernon Murphy orders."

"What makes you say that?" the chief demanded.

"He had nothing to gain by killing his boss or sending a cop to kill his lawyer. Asher stood to lose money if Angeline and Lowell divorced. Getting rid of the girlfriend, Zoey Bertrand, could have been the first step to make sure that didn't happen. But then I showed up to take Vernon back to Montana to stand trial. If I'm right and Asher hired Vernon, he couldn't have him testifying. Have you talked to Jonathan Asher?" He saw the answer on the chief's face.

"It appears he might have left the country," Landry said under his breath.

Willie nodded. "It makes sense. Asher had Vernon abducted and convinced him to keep his mouth shut and keep working for him. Lowell must have figured it out. Asher had to get rid of him, and apparently Vernon as well."

"Let's say you're right. Where does Attorney Phillip McNamara fit into all this?" the chief asked.

"I suspect McNamara wasn't the target." Bile rose in his throat. "The shooter was supposed to kill Attorney E.L. Shafer."

Landry shook his head. "For what possible reason? I can't believe merely because she'd represented Vernon Murphy."

"No," Willie said. "At first I thought she was in danger because whoever hired Vernon would worry about what he told his lawyer. But in truth? She was in danger because of me. I dragged her into all of this." He was the reason she'd almost been killed.

He realized that Asher must have wanted to know what Vernon had told her—just as Phillip McNamara had wanted to know. But Willie didn't think they had wanted to kill her the night outside the pub. That was why they were going to drug her. Otherwise, the man in the alley that day could have easily killed her.

"It wasn't until she started helping me that her life was in danger," he said, feeling the gut-wrenching truth of it in his soul.

Landry shook his head. "What a hero."

"I should have figured it out sooner. If I had…" He didn't like to think how close Ellie had come to dying because he hadn't.

The chief motioned for the officer with him to stop the video recording. "I told you that you can't go around acting on your own." He began to read Willie his rights. "Once you're out of here, you're going to jail—if not prison." With that, the two cops left.

Before his brothers were allowed back in, two federal agents entered his room, making him groan. Willie repeated everything he'd told the chief of police, starting again with what had happened since he'd come to Seattle up to the grand finale in front of Ellie's apartment building.

"Just the whisper of a divorce had Lowell Carter's investors worried. From the get-go, I wasn't sure I could trust the cops. I didn't know then who had tipped off the men who attacked me and took Vernon."

"You believe you were set up."

"From the start," Willie told the agents. "Find Jonathan Asher and you'll find the man behind this whole mess. The chief said it appears he's left the country?"

"It does appear that way," one of the agents said. "We've taken Ms. Shafer's statement. She said you saved her life."

"She's wrong. I risked her life and almost got her killed. She's the one who saved mine."

Chapter Twenty-One

Eleanor pulled on her suit jacket and checked herself in the full-length mirror. She straightened her blouse collar before meeting her reflected gaze squarely. On the surface it would appear that last week hadn't happened, that this was just another workday, that everything about her life was the same.

She was still an attorney at the firm her parents had started, only now she was in power. To her shock, the majority of the senior partners hadn't liked the way Phillip McNamara had been running things. They'd been planning to get him out. Some of the senior partners had been the first ones her parents had hired. Loyal to the family, they'd voted for her to take Phillip's place. The news had come as a shock.

She'd dreamed of seeing her family name again on the masthead. More importantly, she'd dreamed of seeing the firm change and had fought for it with Phillip always shutting her down. Now she could hire female attorneys. She could turn the firm into what she knew it could be.

So, why wasn't she more excited now that it had

happened? It wasn't just the way it had come about, with Phillip's death. She felt an ache low in her belly. Willie Colt. He'd ridden into her life, changed everything and then left, leaving a hole she'd been trying hard to ignore.

Admittedly, he hadn't simply left. His brothers had taken him home to mend. She'd wanted to go with him, but with the crisis at the firm, she'd had no choice but to stay in Seattle. Not that Willie had wanted her with him. If anything, he'd seemed happy to be leaving, as if he wanted to put this all behind him—her included.

"It's for the best," he'd said that day when he was released from the hospital. "Your life is here. Mine's in Montana." She'd seen him swallow, his blue eyes filled with regret? "I'm sorry about so much."

She hadn't known what to say. She hadn't been sorry about anything to do with him. Instead, she'd felt heartbroken.

Eleanor straightened. She had responsibilities. Being managing partner was what she'd worked so hard for all this time. She knew she could run the firm. She'd certainly watched her parents do it her entire life. So, basically, nothing had changed, she told herself.

Except she was no longer the woman Deputy Willie Colt had met that day at her office. She was stronger because of everything she'd been through. Stronger for having met Willie Colt, for loving him.

Before she stepped away from the mirror, she slipped the top button of her blouse free. She was also no longer the buttoned-up attorney, thanks to Willie Colt.

"Now what?" James asked Willie once his gunshot wound had healed. "I heard Sheriff Henson stopped by?"

"To offer me my job back after he heard that I'm running against him in the next election for sheriff," Willie said.

"You're running for sheriff?" This was news to him.

"At least Henson thinks I am." Willie winked and smiled that devilish grin of his. It was good to have him back. They'd all missed him, even when he'd been back in Lonesome for weeks. He just hadn't been himself.

And still wasn't. There was something different about his older brother. He'd lost something out in Seattle. They all knew it had been his heart. James knew firsthand how that could hurt. He worried that his brother might never get over what had happened in the big city. He knew it had little to do with almost dying and a whole lot more to do with falling for the sexy attorney.

Ellie had called every day for a while, then once a week. Her calls had slowly dropped off since Willie hadn't been taking them. James had kept her up-to-date on his brother's recovery. They'd both pretended that was all she'd called about.

"You should reach out to her," James said now, even though neither had mentioned her name.

Willie's smile instantly disappeared, making James regret that he'd said anything. "Thanks for the advice, little brother."

"You can't pretend that nothing happened out there."

"I have the scars to always remind me."

"It's the scars we can't see that I'm talking about. Willie—" His words fell on deaf ears.

His brother got to his feet. "I got a call from a wrecking yard outside of Missoula. I might have found Dad's wrecked pickup. I know it's a long shot…"

"You're sure you want to see it?" James asked. Willie was clearly at loose ends, which was why he'd been investigating their father's death with a vengeance. None of them believed it had been an accident, but thanks to the sloppy work of then sheriff Otis Osterman, they'd never been able to prove it.

"If there is any chance that evidence was overlooked…"

James worried that his brother was in for more disappointment. He was so glad that Willie was feeling better. He didn't want to lose him again to that dark place he'd been in for weeks after returning from Seattle. "It's been almost ten years. What evidence could there still be?"

Willie shrugged. "I have some free time before I win the election. What else do I have to do?"

"I like your confidence. But you probably can't beat Sheriff Henson," James said with a laugh. "So you know you're welcome to come to work with us. We keep getting more investigative jobs all the time."

His brother shook his head. "Thanks, but if I don't win the sheriff seat, I'm not sure what I'm going to do yet. But don't worry about me." He patted James on the shoulder as he started out the door. "I'll call you if I find anything."

James couldn't help but worry about his older brother.

Willie had healed nicely, Doc had said, but James had
seen the change in him. As Willie had improved, Ellie
had wanted to come to Lonesome, but James hadn't
encouraged her. He knew it was the last thing Willie
wanted.

"What's going on with you and Ellie?" he'd asked
his brother once Willie had started feeling better.

"Nothing." Willie had gotten that closed-off look
he always did when it was something he didn't want
to talk about.

"She's worried about you." No reaction. "Did something happen between the two of you?"

"I almost got her killed, that's what happened," his
brother had snapped. "I was so determined to solve the
damned case." He shook his head. "I should never have
gone out there. I should never have…" He looked away.

James knew how stubborn the Colt men could be.
"You do realize that she's in love with you, right?"

"She'll get over it."

James had chuckled. "But will you?"

Willie had rolled over. "I need to rest. Close the door
on your way out."

He'd left him alone and hadn't brought up Ellie
again. But he couldn't help feeling bad for both of them.
He remembered too well falling in love with Lori and
how painful it had been until he'd opened up his heart
to her and let her in.

Maybe there wasn't any hope for Willie and Ellie.
Willie certainly wasn't going to move to Seattle, and
according to his brother, she was now responsible for

the firm her parents had built. Her life was in the big city and Willie Colt was no big-city cowboy.

It broke his heart because he could tell that a lot of his brother's pain had nothing to do with the gunshot wound.

ELEANOR LOOKED AROUND the office, missing her old one. The views of Seattle and the Sound and even Mount Rainier were incredible up here. She could understand why Phillip had wanted to hang on to it so badly.

She still didn't know how deeply he'd been involved with the Vernon Murphy case. Enough that it had gotten him killed? Or had those bullets been for her? She would never know. She suspected Willie knew, but he wasn't about to tell her. He wouldn't even talk to her when she called.

Pushing that thought away, she considered the remodel she'd had done on the office. There was nothing to remind her of Phillip and yet it felt as if he was still here—just as she felt her parents and had since law school. This was what they had always wanted for her. They would have been pleased, she thought.

But as she stood looking out at the Sound, her thoughts always turned to Willie. She'd talked to James earlier.

"I'm sorry, Ellie, he's not here. He got a call about our father's pickup being found at a wrecking yard in Missoula. He drove down to see if even after all these years, there was some evidence still in it."

"Sounds like him," she said, her voice betraying

how much she missed him. He'd thrown himself into solving his father's death. "Determination isn't something he lacks."

"How are you doing? Enjoying your new office and position at the firm?"

"It's been busy. I never knew what the job entailed. Corralling attorneys feels like herding cats, not to mention trying to keep the partners happy. They seem to think I should have all the answers."

"I'm sure you're doing a great job." The conversation had died off and she'd said she had a meeting and got off the line. It was too painful talking to James. She kept remembering the night she'd spent in his and Lori's beautiful, cozy home on Colt Ranch. Lying in bed that night with Willie, she'd felt as if she'd belonged in Lonesome, belonged with the cowboy.

She walked back to her desk, hating the tears that burned her eyes. Willie had made his lack of intentions clear. His job in Seattle was over—and so were the two of them. Not that they had ever put a name to what they'd been. Lovers? Friends? Coconspirators? Colleagues?

Definitely lovers, she thought with that old ache. She'd hoped the pain would have gone away by now. Her friends encouraged her to date, but she had no interest. She knew there was no one out there like Willie Colt. And he was all that she wanted.

She got a message. The partners were waiting for her in the boardroom.

Chapter Twenty-Two

The wrecking yard was huge. Willie had seen the rows and rows of old beaters miles away. It had taken him weeks of calling junkyards for fifty miles around Lonesome before he'd finally found his father's pickup.

"You're sure the plates on the pickup match?" he'd asked when an older man had called him back to say he thought he had the pickup Willie was looking for.

"Yep. Hit by a train, right?"

"Right," Willie said, grimacing inside at the thought of what he was going to see when he found it.

"A 2010 blue-and-white crew-cab Ford."

"That's it." He couldn't believe that he'd actually tracked it down. "I'm on my way." He'd hung up, telling himself not to get his hopes up. It had been ten years since his father's death. All that time the pickup had been sitting out in the elements. If there had been any evidence, it would be gone.

Yet nothing could keep him from going to see it. He knew it wouldn't be easy, a crash like that, knowing that his father had been inside that pickup when the train collided with it. But it was something he had to do. He didn't trust that former sheriff Otis Osterman had done a thorough investigation of the crash.

If anything, Willie suspected Otis would have covered up evidence. The sheriff had never liked any of the Colts, maybe especially their father, Del. Otis had been convinced that Del had been drunk and that was why he'd stopped on the railroad track with the train coming.

Willie and his brothers had never believed that, even though Otis swore he saw their father arguing with a woman outside a bar not long before the train wreck. Del had an occasional paper cup of blackberry brandy, but that was it. True, he'd been involved in a difficult case involving the hit-and-run death of a young boy. The coroner's report showed that Del had consumed some alcohol, but it wasn't over the legal limit at the time of his death, even though Otis also swore that an empty bottle of whiskey had been found at the accident site.

There were too many unanswered questions. But their father knew how dangerous that railroad crossing was. He'd always warned his sons about it. Where had he been going that night?

Willie couldn't help but hope that some of those answers might still be in his father's pickup as he drove to the small town outside of Missoula.

A skinny, weathered man somewhere in his late seventies came out of the small shack-like office as Willie drove up to the wrecking yard. He wore faded blue overalls over a red plaid flannel shirt and muck boots.

"Clyde Stanley?" Willie asked.

Pushing back the grimy trucker's cap on his gray head, Clyde gave Willie a nod and pointed to the south. Without a word, the older man headed out. Willie followed through this graveyard of abandoned vehicles. The wind whistled through the torn metal, kicking up dust, sending a stray tumbleweed blowing between the rows.

The pickup was on the side of a windswept hill, between an old Cadillac with fins and a smashed-in front and a van missing its engine.

Willie spotted the pickup and stopped walking. He stood a few yards away and had to swallow back the bile that rose in his throat. He'd seen wrecked vehicles after being hit by trains before, but they hadn't had his father inside. He took a deep breath and let it out.

"I can take it from here," he said, looking to his right, only to find that Clyde Stanley had already gone back to his office, leaving him entirely alone. The wind seemed to pick up as he approached the vehicle, whirling dust and dirt around him.

He tamped down any emotion, drawing on his strengths. It wouldn't be the first time he'd had to "cowboy up." It was something their father had taught them at a young age. Willie remembered his first rodeo. He couldn't have been much over two. He'd tried to ride one of the sheep. He'd fallen off, gotten trampled and his face pushed into the dirt.

Hurt and crying, he'd gone to his father. Del had checked him over, seen that he wasn't hurt badly and told him there was no crying. "If you're going to do this, you have to learn to 'cowboy up.' Later you can lick your wounds, but in the arena, you keep a stiff upper lip. Show them who you are. You're a Colt." He never forgot. His father's advice had gotten him through some tough times.

None had been tougher than what he'd gone through in Seattle. Just the thought of Ellie made his heart ache. That pain had to be far worse than seeing how and where his father had died. As he walked over to the pickup, he rubbed his healing shoulder and told himself he could do this.

The train had apparently hit the front part of the Ford, pushing the engine almost out the other side. It had also smashed in the driver's side, the metal buckling, with the steering wheel facing the passenger seat.

But rather than push the pickup down the tracks, the train had flipped it off to the side. Because of that, the passenger side hadn't been as badly damaged. He tried the door, but it refused to open. The crew-cab door directly behind it opened with a groan. The grinding sound was chillingly loud.

His father never carried much in the back seats. They looked almost brand-new. He peered over the front passenger seat to what had landed on the floorboard. In the police report he'd read a variety of items had been taken from the pickup. Tools, a handgun, a shotgun, some paperwork and reportedly a whiskey bottle.

Now all he could see was dirt that had blown in to form small dunes. Out of the corner of his eye, he saw the stained fabric of the front seat. He leaned back, swallowing hard, and looked at the back seat floor. Lots of broken glass, some stained with a dark smear that he knew was also blood.

What had he hoped to find after all this time? He leaned against the seat, the wind howling through the missing window glass, and took a breath. There were no answers here. Not to why his father was on that road that night. Not to why he would have stopped on the railroad track. Not to his father's state of mind.

Maybe he had been drinking. Maybe the Billy Sherman case hit too close to home with his own sons. Unfortunately, Willie feared they would never know.

He started to turn away when he caught a glint of gold snagged at the edge of the door behind the passenger seat. He stared, thinking he was seeing things. It appeared to be a gold, horseshoe-shaped charm.

Reaching down, he tried to pick it up. That was when he saw that there was a thin gold chain attached. He pulled out his pocketknife and worked the chain out of the crack. Parts of the chain and charm were tarnished from the weather and the years. Holding it in the palm of his hand, he realized it was a little girl's necklace.

He frowned. What was it doing in his father's pickup? He rubbed his thumb over the charm attached to the tiny chain and saw that a name had been engraved inside the horseshoe.

DelRae.

Chapter Twenty-Three

On his way back to Lonesome, Willie called his brothers and told them to meet him at the office. All three were waiting when he walked in. He could tell by their expressions that they were hoping he'd found the evidence they'd all been anxious for. He hated to disappoint them.

He wished at least one of them could help explain the little girl's necklace as he pulled it out of his jeans pocket and put it on his father's desk between them.

"What is this?" James asked, picking it up and holding it in the light. "Is that…" He was squinting at the engraving.

"DelRae. It's a girl's name," Willie said. "I found it on the floorboard of Dad's pickup."

James passed the necklace to Tommy, who studied it and passed it on to Davy. "I don't get it," Davy said.

"Neither do I," Willie said. "But you have to admit, it's too much of a coincidence. Dad's name is Del Ransom Colt."

"Not DelRae," Tommy pointed out.

"But close," Willie argued. "What if Otis Osterman

was telling the truth about Dad arguing with a woman outside the bar that night?"

"This necklace looks like a child's—not a woman's," Davy said, dropping it back on the desk.

"Like the kind a parent might buy for a daughter," Willie said.

James sat down at their father's old desk. "Wait, what are you getting at?"

"What was the necklace doing in Dad's pickup?" Willie said. "What if there was a woman from Dad's past—and a child?"

"Slow down. Let's not jump to conclusions based on a tarnished piece of jewelry," James said, and paused. "I admit, though…the name DelRae does make me wonder, especially the odd way it's spelled."

"It's an unusual enough name that if there is some-one out there…" Tommy had already stepped to his computer and was tapping away at the keys. "Would help if we had a last name."

Willie heard his brother curse. "What did you find?" he asked as he moved to Tommy's desk.

"There is no DelRae Colt, but Dad could have had other kids," Tommy said. His brothers looked at him but no one spoke. Their father had had another relationship none of them knew about? Del Ransom Colt wasn't one to have secrets. The question was, if they were wrong about that, did they want to know those secrets?

"How would we find DelRae?" Davy asked. "If she exists?"

"And are we sure we want to?" James said, voicing what they had all been thinking.

"What if she's the answer to what really happened that night on the railroad tracks?" Willie said. His cell phone rang. He checked it, already knowing it wouldn't be Ellie—not after he hadn't been taking her calls. Talking to her would hurt too much.

He could never let himself forget that he'd almost gotten her killed. As much as it hurt to end their relationship the way he had, he told himself it was for her own good. Her life was in Seattle. His was in Lonesome, Montana. What more was there to say?

His cell rang again. It was a number he didn't recognize. He could feel his brothers watching him with growing disapproval. They thought it might be Ellie.

He answered. A woman's voice told him the Federal Bureau of Investigations office was calling and to please hold while she connected the call.

"It's the FBI," he said as he took the call.

ELEANOR HAD SPENT the past few days in meetings. She felt exhausted, but glad she was finally free to do some work of her own, when her assistant buzzed her.

"Mrs. Carter is here to see you," she said.

She sighed. "Mrs. Carter didn't have an appointment, did she?" For some time now, she'd felt distressed, especially when her mind wandered to Willie.

"Also, Police Chief Landry is here. He insists it can't wait."

Groaning silently, she said, "Have Mrs. Carter wait. I'll see Landry first."

Eleanor assumed the man had stopped by with news about Jonathan Asher. Why he'd share it with her, though, was questionable. Willie had suspected the man who resembled a bulldog had known more about Vernon Murphy's abduction than he wanted anyone to know. That was enough to make her nervous as the short, stocky man entered her office.

WILLIE'S FIRST THOUGHT was that the feds had found Jonathan Asher. When an agent came on the line, he listened, thanked the man for calling, and disconnected.

Looking up to find his brothers anxiously waiting to hear what was up, he said, "Jonathan Asher. They found his body. They're treating it as a homicide." He swallowed and then dropped the real bombshell. "The last time Asher was seen alive was the night Alex Mattson visited him."

"What are you saying?" James said.

"There's a good chance that he couldn't have been behind the killings because he was already dead," Willie said, his mind whirling. Someone had made it appear that Asher had packed up and left the country. If he was already dead… "That means I was wrong. It means…" He pulled out his phone and hurriedly called Ellie.

"I'M AFRAID I have a busy day ahead of me, Chief Landry," she said, not wanting to offer him a chair, hoping whatever he had to say would be quick.

But he took a seat anyway and looked around her office for a few moments before he finally spoke. "Nice view." It made her think of the first time she'd met Willie. He hadn't been all that impressed by her office or the view; he'd just been suspicious of whoever had hired her to defend Vernon Murphy.

Eleanor lowered herself into her chair, seeing that this wasn't going to be quick. "What can I do for you, Chief Landry?"

"Just thought you'd want to know," the man said in his gravelly voice. "The DNA report came back on that second body believed to have been Vernon Murphy's in the warehouse after the explosion." He met her gaze. "It wasn't his." He nodded as if seeing her surprise. "Vernon's still out there."

She recovered quickly from the startling and worrisome news. "I'm sure you are actively looking for him. Just as you are for Jonathan Asher." Why was this man sitting across from her right now, wasting time on the taxpayer's dollar?

"Thing is, we still have a killer on the loose. Got me thinking. You were Vernon's lawyer. Shared a lot of secrets, I bet. I asked myself, who benefited from all this?" He looked around her office again, glancing out the floor-to-ceiling windows to the glittering city below. "Look at you in this snazzy office. Things turned out pretty good for you, didn't they?"

The chief was right about one thing. She'd benefited from Phillip's death. Sighing, she looked around the office. It was gorgeous and everything she'd ever dreamed of having. Now the accomplishment felt hollow.

Her father had made no secret about wanting her to make it on her own. He'd wanted her to work her way up in the firm to partner, then managing partner. He'd trusted Phillip, a mistake they'd both made.

Her cell phone rang. She picked it up, surprised to see that it was Willie Colt calling. Her pulse jumped. Why was he calling? Had something happened? He'd made it clear that the two of them had nothing more to say to each other. Why call after all this time?

She looked up at the chief of police. "Are we about finished here, Chief Landry?"

"Do you still carry a gun, Ms. Shafer?" the chief asked.

Trying to hide her irritation, she declined the call and said, "No, I don't have a gun." She doubted she ever would again. The police had taken the one Willie had given her, the one she'd used to wound Officer Alex Mattson. The coroner had ruled that Mattson's death was due to heavy trauma when hit by a truck.

The chief nodded, openly studying her. The department had taken a blow that she doubted Landry would get over soon. "You don't seem all that concerned to hear that Vernon is still alive," Landry said. "Why is that?"

"I have no reason to be concerned."

He raised a brow, a smile pulling at his lips. "So you did get close to Vernon." His smile broadened. "Then again, while you might know his secrets, I'm wondering if he knows a few of yours. You that sure Vernon doesn't have a reason to want you dead, Ms. Shafer?"

She'd represented Vernon like she had her other clients. He hadn't wanted to be extradited and had begged her to find a way to keep him in jail in Washington.

She hadn't been able to. Would he blame her if he really was still alive?

Eleanor cleared her throat and rose. "Chief Landry, I have work to do. Unless you've come here to arrest me…"

He locked gazes with her as if he thought he could intimidate her. He wasn't the first to try. He looked away as he slowly rose from the chair. "Don't let me keep you, then."

She watched him amble out the door and waited, listening for the elevator. She told herself that he was trying to scare her. She told herself that he was angry with Willie, and her as well, because of everything that had happened. They'd made the local police look inept.

She looked out at the rainy morning. Even the rain annoyed her now, she thought as she watched the latest storm streak the windows and blur her view. This had been her dream. *But dreams change*, she thought as she went back to her desk and tried to call Willie. The call went straight to voice mail. Maybe the call had been accidental. She didn't leave a message.

She realized that she'd forgotten all about Angeline Carter and hurriedly messaged her assistant.

I didn't want to interrupt while you were with the police chief, but Mrs. Carter said she couldn't stay and that she would catch you later, came the reply.

With Phillip gone, Angeline would probably be moving her business to another firm. That was probably why she'd stopped by, Eleanor thought as she tried to go back to work.

She kept thinking about Willie. What if it had been

something important? She started to try his number again, but stopped. She'd called and left too many messages over the past few months, she thought shamefully. It was pathetic, her attempts to reach him.

WILLIE SNATCHED UP his phone without even checking to see who was calling. "Ellie?" He hadn't heard her voice in weeks. He'd thought he'd never hear it again. As part of his healing, he'd tried to put Seattle and the attorney into the past. The gunshot wound had been painful, but nothing like letting go of Ellie.

"It's James. Are you at the airport?"

"I just got here. I hope she calls before I board," he said.

"She probably tried to call you back," his brother said. "There's minimal cell service through the canyon."

He hoped his brother was right. He wouldn't blame Ellie if she never wanted to speak to him again. Since hearing about Jonathan Asher's remains being found, he was more than anxious to talk to her. He'd been frantically trying to put the pieces together. If not Asher, if not Lowell Carter, if not Vernon, if not Alex Mattson, then who the hell was behind this?

"Keep in touch. If Ellie calls here, I'll tell her you're on your way to see her," James said.

He thanked his brother, who'd spoken more to Ellie than he had the past few months. Just the sound of her voice made him hurt worse. Yet, every day he'd wanted to pick up the phone and call her and tell her how he felt about her.

There had to be some way to work this out. But then

he would remind himself that he'd almost gotten her killed and all the other reasons they couldn't be together.

It would never work out, he kept reminding himself. Neither of them could survive in the other's environment. Ellie was a city girl. He was all country. She would hate Lonesome even if she found it quaint at first. There was no way he could navigate Seattle with all its traffic and people. He'd be miserable, and eventually they would resent each other. Nothing could kill love quicker.

He'd watched his brothers fall in love and almost lose the women they loved. He'd been determined never to feel that kind of pain by never falling in love. Love. He swore. He didn't even know if Ellie had felt the same way he did.

Good thing he hadn't bared his soul to her. What if she had been horrified by his confession? Or, worse, laughed before gently letting him down? He wasn't the kind of man she dated. The last thing she needed was a cowboy who didn't fit into her life.

He'd almost deleted her number from his phone. He was thankful now that he hadn't. But he should have left a message earlier. He heard his flight called and decided to try her office number.

HER ASSISTANT MESSAGED that Willie Colt was on the line and that it was urgent.

Chief Landry's visit had made her more nervous than she wanted to admit. Learning that Vernon was possibly still alive…

She quickly took the call, no longer pretending that

she didn't want to hear his voice. She tried to tamp down the hope that soared inside her.

"This is Eleanor," she said into the phone in her most formal tone.

"Ellie," he said. "It wasn't Asher."

She hadn't known what to expect, so it was no wonder that the words made no sense. "What?"

"I'm about to get on a flight to Seattle, so I don't have time to explain it all, but Jonathan Asher was murdered *before* the warehouse was blown up, *before* Lowell and Vernon died. He was apparently one of the victims."

Just the sound of Willie's voice sent a spike of regret and desire through her. But it was the other feeling that hurt the most. She'd fallen in love with this cowboy. Tears burned her eyes. He'd called about the case. Of course it wasn't personal, just as she'd suspected. All he cared about was the case, so she said, "Vernon. The DNA. It wasn't his."

"I'm on my way out there," he said as if he already knew that or didn't hear. "If I miss you at work, I'll meet you at your apartment. Ellie?"

"Yes?" She held her breath waiting for him to say the words she'd yearned for—or anything close to *I love you.*

"I have to go or I'm going to miss my flight. Just be careful." He disconnected and she sat holding the phone. Tears welled and fell. She wiped at them. Angry with herself for the hope that had been so quickly smothered. Why would she foolishly think he would tell her he loved her after his silence the past few months? What was wrong with her?

Slowly she hung up the phone she was still holding. He'd caught her flat-footed. She'd hoped the call was about them. Instead, it was about the case?

Now he was on his way to Seattle? Willie was on his way to her. She couldn't do it, she told herself, even as she felt her heart bump in her chest at the thought of seeing him again. Elation mixed with dread at what was coming. It would be starting all over again. The fear. Willie back in her life—but only temporarily and only if one or both of them didn't get killed.

But if Jonathan Asher hadn't orchestrated everything... Vernon? No one thought he was smart enough, but what if they were wrong? What if he was behind everything—including making it appear he'd died in the last building he'd destroyed?

She shuddered. Would he have reason to come after her?

Eleanor tried to concentrate on work, losing herself in legal paperwork as she had for years. It wasn't until her assistant announced she was leaving for the day that she realized she actually had lost herself for a while in her work. She looked to the wall of windows overlooking the city. The rain appeared to have stopped, though the sky was still gray with low hanging clouds.

She'd thought she would see Willie here when he arrived, keep it cordial, but she couldn't bear to wait here in this office. She rose, retrieved her coat and purse, and started for the door, then turned back. Picking up the phone, she called downstairs.

Herb, her favorite security guard, answered. "I'm

expecting Mr. Colt to stop by. I'm headed down to the
parking level. If I miss him, would you please tell him
I'll be at my apartment?" Herb said he would be happy
to.

Willie's short flight from Montana should have
landed by now. She didn't want to think about what
might happen between the two of them at her apartment. Or, worse, what might not happen.

Taking the elevator to the parking level, she almost
talked herself into returning to her office. Even her
apartment wasn't the same since Willie had burst into
her life. She felt him everywhere, as if he was always
with her now, deep in her heart.

The elevator shuddered and slowed as it neared the
parking garage. Something clanked. A chill curled
around her neck. The police chief had managed to put
her on edge about Vernon. Landry would have been
delighted to know that, she thought, and shoved away
her discomfort.

She wondered if the chief had only come by her office to scare her. Landry wanted something on Willie
Colt, that much was obvious. But there had been too
much blowback on the police department once it was
discovered that Alex Mattson had been involved. Also,
it hadn't helped that Willie had solved the case—not
the big-city law enforcement. It probably didn't hurt
that the FBI had been involved or that she had said
she would represent Willie if the Seattle police came
after him. No charges had been filed on either of them.

She felt the elevator shudder to a stop on the parking
level. As the door opened, the sound echoed through

the nearly empty space. She saw a shadow fall across the concrete floor in front of the elevator. For one delusional moment, she thought it was Willie, but could he have made it from the airport already?

It wasn't Willie who suddenly filled the elevator's open doorway. Eleanor was so startled when she recognized the person that she didn't react fast enough. She no longer had a gun in her purse, but she did have pepper spray—a gift from Willie he'd had his brothers purchase for her before he'd left.

Unfortunately, she didn't have time to get to it before the business end of a gun was shoved into her face and she was pushed back into the elevator.

"Let's go up on the roof. The view is breathtaking."

Chapter Twenty-Four

As the elevator rose toward the rooftop, Eleanor tried to catch her breath. Her heart thundered in her chest even as she told herself that this wasn't happening. She'd been through so much. This couldn't be how it ended—not with Willie on his way. Just the thought that she might never see him again…

She leaned against the elevator wall for support as she shifted her gaze from the gun to the woman holding it. "Mrs. Carter, what do you—"

"For crying out loud," Angeline Carter snapped. "Don't you think we should be on a first-name basis by now?"

She swallowed. "I don't understand what's going on."

"It's pretty simple. We're going up on the roof and you're going to jump."

A shiver ran the length of her spine. The woman appeared deadly serious. "Why would I do that?"

"Because you can't live with yourself after everything that has happened. First Phillip, then that cowboy breaking your heart."

"He didn't break my heart," she said as if that mattered right now.

"Oh, I know a broken heart when I see one. Lowell wasn't the first man who broke mine. Did you know that Phil and I used to be lovers?"

She shook her head.

"I talked him into investing in the mining business when Lowell was first getting it off the ground."

"Phillip never mentioned that." She realized how little she'd known about Phillip's...dealings, but she now suspected that was what had gotten him killed.

Angeline seemed to be studying her. "He didn't tell you I asked him to give you the Vernon Murphy case?"

Eleanor couldn't help her confusion with a gun pointed at her and this clearly unbalanced woman telling her she was about to jump off the roof of the office building. "Why would you do that?"

"Phillip, you silly twit. Weren't you listening?" Angeline spat and Eleanor realized that she hadn't been. Willie had said he would be here soon. Would he know how to find her, though? What if he went to her apartment first? Or Herb told him she'd already left?

"Phillip and I were more than lovers. We confided in each other. He told me about his affair with your mother."

"I really doubt—"

"He dumped me for her. But when I told your father about the two of them..." She smiled a cat-who-ate-the-canary smile. "I've always wondered if they were arguing about me when they had the car wreck that killed them. Or maybe it wasn't an accident at all."

Eleanor thought she'd be sick to her stomach. She had suspected her father hadn't been faithful, but her mother? Now this woman was insinuating the wreck that had killed them might not have been an accident? When she spoke, her voice was calm, and yet her heart thumped wildly in her chest. "Why are you telling me this?"

"Because we have so much in common. Phillip told me that he was in love with you. I knew he wanted you, since he couldn't have your mother. But I had no idea he felt so…strongly." The woman's words dripped with bitterness. *Hell hath no fury like a woman scorned.* "Then there was Lowell. He actually thought I was going to divorce him and let him walk away with half of what I'd built."

Eleanor fought to make sense of this. "I thought—"

"I just wanted Lowell to think I was divorcing him. I made Lowell. I got him the financing to start the business, I hosted the parties for investors and people in high places who would grease the wheels and also look the other way if necessary." Her voice rose with her anger, echoing in the small space. "I built that company. Not Lowell. I was fine with people believing I knew nothing about his business. But it was all me. He thought I was going to let him walk away with half of everything I'd built so he could be with that tart?" Her laugh held no humor.

The elevator came to a stop. The door opened. Angeline motioned with the gun. Eleanor felt a tremor of fear as the damp night air rushed in. *Keep her talking.* She didn't move. The last thing she wanted to do was step out this door and onto the open roof twenty floors above the city. She could feel the wind, strong up here, heavy with the scent of the Sound.

"You were the one who hired Vernon Murphy to destroy the building with Zoey Bertrand in it."

Angeline touched the tip of her nose with her free hand as she smiled. "Vernon has worked for me for years. I make sure he gets what he needs—a building to blow up here and there and he's as loyal as an old dog."

This sweet-faced, tiny woman who'd been wearing the guise of a victim was a heartless killer. "You killed Phillip."

"Me? I thought he was killed in a drive-by shooting. The man Vernon got for me wasn't much of a shot, since he was supposed to take out both of you—and your cowboy cop friend, too, if he was with you."

"Why?" Eleanor told herself that this made no sense. She understood why Angeline wanted her husband and his mistress dead. But her attorney?

Angeline's smile was all shark teeth. "Phillip was fine giving you Vernon's case as a favor to me—until it got dangerous. Then he started making threats. I had to remind him that I knew things about him—like the way he'd gotten control of this firm after your parents died. Bet you always wondered how he managed that."

Eleanor said nothing. Phillip had been the son her father never had. She'd just assumed her father had believed he would build the firm—just as he had—and make a place for Eleanor in it.

"Once you took off with that cowboy cop, he was

beside himself with worry about you," Angeline said. "That's when I knew how deep his feelings were for you. He didn't have to tell me how much you're like your mother, but he did. I can't count all the times Phillip told me what a hellion you were when it came to the courtroom. Focused, cool, calm, calculated and brilliant. A true fighter, just like your mother. I knew you couldn't be bought off or dissuaded with reason or threats. I knew there was only one way to stop you—and your cowboy. I was going to have to kill you both—and Phillip, too, just like I did your mother."

Eleanor stared at her, unable to speak. "She was killed in a car wreck. How could you—"

"I grew up in a mining camp around equipment. Fixing the brakes to fail on your mother's car was child's play for me."

Her heart drummed in her chest, her stomach roiling. "Phillip knew."

Angeline's laugh was brittle as an old windowpane. "I'd always been able to hold what I knew about Phillip over his head, but he was threatening to tell you the truth—and to turn me in."

Eleanor shook her head. She'd had no idea what had been going on between her parents and Phillip. "So this is personal, an old grudge against my mother." This woman had already killed before. And would kill again, she reminded herself. There would be nothing stopping her.

Unless Eleanor could distract her long enough to get to the pepper spray.

"Of course it's personal," Angeline snapped, and motioned for Eleanor to get out of the elevator. "Especially since Phillip had decided to go to the authorities. Said I'd gone too far too many times. He wasn't going to let me destroy you the way I had your mother. Now get out. Don't think I won't shoot you where you stand."

WILLIE'D HAD JAMES hire him an Uber for when his plane landed. By the time he got out of the terminal, a car was waiting for him. The driver had the address of Ellie's apartment building, but Willie realized she would still be at work. He gave the driver the law firm's address instead.

He could feel time slipping away too quickly. The flight from Missoula, Montana, to Seattle had been short once they were in the air. It was all the other wasted time that went with flying that drove him to distraction. He'd had too much time to think.

Mulling it all over, he saw now that he'd been a coward. He should have told Ellie how he felt. He'd had plenty of opportunities, but the longer they were apart while his gunshot wound healed, the more he'd talked himself out of it.

He promised himself that no matter how she felt, he would tell her the truth. He'd fallen in love with her. It had taken him a long time to admit it. Because everything was too complicated, he told himself. Love didn't solve the fact that they lived miles away from each other in very different worlds. Love didn't solve the fact that his job—if he won the election for sheriff—was dangerous. He'd be dragging her into trouble even if he didn't mean to.

Nor did love bridge the divide between the different paths they'd taken in this life so far.

So, why tell her that he loved her when there was no hope for a future for them?

Because he couldn't hold it in his heart any longer without admitting the truth. He loved her. And if she didn't love him…

The car stopped in front of her office building. He leaped out and ran toward the front door. The security guard was at his desk.

"I have to see Ellie… E.L. Shafer," he said as he ran toward the elevator. Short of the guard shooting him, nothing could stop him.

"She's not in her office," the man called as Willie hit the elevator button. The door opened and he stepped in, then stopped.

"She already went home?"

The guard shook his head. "She told me to watch for you. She was headed for her apartment, she said, but she didn't get out on the parking level. Instead, she must have changed her mind. I saw the elevator open, but she didn't get out. I had to take a call. When I looked again, the elevator was headed up to the roof. It's stopped up there."

He'd already hit the button for the top floor, the elevator door closing, before he realized what the guard had said. The roof. The elevator shot upward. Ellie had been planning to go to her apartment, but once she reached the parking garage, she changed her mind? Why would she suddenly decide to go up on the roof?

Because she wasn't alone.

ELEANOR LOOKED INTO the woman's eyes. Angeline was intent on killing her, one way or another. There was nothing squeamish about her. Maybe she hadn't killed anyone face-to-face before, but she'd sure plotted the killings of others, including her husband and her former lover. And if she was telling the truth, the murders of Eleanor's own mother and father.

"Won't shooting me be hard to explain to the authorities?" she asked, stalling for time as she tried to come up with a plan for survival. Herb would know that the elevator to the roof was stopped up here. He would eventually investigate.

But she feared he would be too late.

"I'm not going to jump," Eleanor said. "You're going to have to kill me here in this elevator."

"Why not? Did you really think I didn't have a backup plan?" Angeline laughed as she raised the gun slightly, leveling it at Eleanor's heart, her hand steady, her finger on the trigger. "You'll die, but I'll only be wounded and manage to call for help. I'll tell the cops it was Vernon who killed you and wounded me."

"You've thought of everything." She could see that it just might work. Angeline didn't look like a killer. That was what had gotten her this far.

With a nod, Eleanor stepped out of the elevator and was instantly buffeted by the wind. Behind her, she heard Angeline release the elevator. The doors closed, and it hummed downward. Herb wouldn't be coming up to check it.

Her fear intensified. She was truly alone on the rooftop with this unbalanced woman. The air felt laden with moisture, the darkness on the rooftop complete. She turned her face up to the night sky, afraid but determined not to die. Not here. Not now. Not with Willie on his way.

Just the thought though made her realize that if he did find her up here, Angeline would gun him down. Eleanor couldn't let that happen any more than she could let this woman push her off this roof.

"If all you wanted was to keep your husband from taking off with his mistress, you accomplished that with Vernon's help," she said as she moved slowly across the massive roof. "Why keep killing?"

The closer she got, the more she could see. There was a short wall around the roof that she estimated was less than three feet high. Anyone could fall over it. For a woman like Angeline, pushing her over that wall would be child's play. She kept talking even though Angeline hadn't responded. "Vernon didn't know Zoey Bertrand would be in the building. Did he threaten to turn on you? Is that why you had him abducted?"

"You *are* smart," Angeline said. "Too bad you aren't as smart as Vernon. It took only a little persuading to get him to see reason once I kept him from being extradited."

Eleanor shook her head. "He's still wanted for arson and murder," she said over her shoulder.

"True, but what's some prison time compared to death?" Angeline jabbed her in the back with the gun, making her stumble forward.

Eleanor could see more of the lights of the city, feel a stronger wind near the edge of the roof, hear traffic below. "You really are an evil mastermind," she said, fighting to keep her tone calm, even complimentary. "My mother must have underestimated you."

"People always do."

"But all these deaths…"

"Come on, you've stalled enough. No one is coming to save you. I waited to make sure that your cowboy had left town. He got to you, didn't he?" She laughed. "Whatever you thought the two of you had, it was all in your mind. I know the feeling."

Eleanor feared she was right. Willie wouldn't be able to save her since only one elevator came all the way up to the roof. The other elevator would only take him to the top floor, from where he would have to take the stairs. He'd never make it in time to save her—or himself.

She was on her own. The thought sent both fear and regret through her. After falling in love for the first time in her life, she couldn't believe it would end like this—not knowing if Willie had felt anything and wondering if it was all in her mind, like Angeline had said.

Her heart was lodged in her throat as the woman pushed her toward the ledge and the twenty-story drop to the pavement below. From this height, cars would look like children's toys, people like ants.

Eleanor told herself that Angeline didn't know Willie Colt. Nor did she know the woman Ellie had become since meeting the cowboy. She turned just a little to look back at Angeline, drawing the woman's attention as she slid her hand into her shoulder bag and closed her fingers around the pepper spray.

She felt the wind in her face and knew that the pepper spray would be worse than worthless up here. It would blow back in her own face, blinding her, making it even easier for Angeline to push her off the roof.

THE ELEVATOR WILLIE had taken didn't go to the rooftop. It opened on the top floor. It took him a few precious minutes to find the stairs to the roof. He scrambled up them, terrified of what he would find once he reached the rooftop.

He told himself that she might not be up here. That even if she was, she might be alone, and there was no need to panic.

But he knew better. She'd been leaving for her apartment. She knew he was coming to Seattle, coming to her. He felt a lump rise in his throat. He was coming back and not just to make sure she was safe, but to tell her what was in his heart.

As he took the stairs three at a time, he prayed he'd get the chance. He'd worked it out on the plane. If Lowell or Jonathan hadn't been behind this and Vernon was still alive...

He reached the door, shoved it open, gun drawn, and saw two figures near the edge of the roof. Ellie and the woman he knew had been behind this the whole time. Angeline Carter. She was shoving Ellie toward the edge of the roof. He started to take a step out when the wind caught the door, jerking it out of his hand.

ELEANOR HEARD A door slam against the wall next to the elevator. Angeline heard it, too, both of them turning to look back. As Willie started to step through it, Eleanor yelled, "She's got a gun!"

Angeline swung the gun toward Willie and fired. The bullet tore into the stucco on the wall next to him, forcing him to duck back inside the stairwell as the elevator she and Angeline had ridden up in dinged. The door opened and a man stepped out. Vernon!

She wasn't the only one who'd looked back. Angeline had been distracted just long enough that Eleanor was able to spin around and grab the woman's wrist holding the gun.

Angeline was petite, small-framed, but much stronger than she looked. As the two wrestled for the weapon, Eleanor found herself being forced back the few yards to the edge of the roof. She could hear the traffic, feel the wind.

The report of a gunshot echoed over the roofline as Eleanor fought to get the gun free. Out of the corner of her eye, she saw that she was getting dangerously close to the edge of the roof. She heard Willie call out her name, heard another shot.

Past Angeline, she saw Vernon rush Willie, barreling into him. She screamed his name as another gunshot filled the air, the handgun bucking in Angeline's hand. The woman smiled without looking back, as if she knew that Vernon would come through for her once again. Eleanor saw Willie stumble as the two fought. She let out a cry as she tried even harder to get the gun away from Angeline.

Shoved back, she tripped into the short wall at the edge of the roof. She quit trying to wrench the gun away and flung a hand back to keep from falling backward into the abyss.

No longer needing the gun, Angeline smiled and tossed it aside as she charged, throwing her whole body into it. In that split second, Eleanor hurled herself to the side, forced to lean out over the edge to miss a direct hit from the crazed woman. She felt Angeline's hand hit her hand, then saw the woman's eyes widen as she realized that instead of hitting Eleanor in the middle of her chest and pushing her over the edge of the roof, she'd only managed to brush her shoulder.

Angeline looked confused when her hand came away with the strap of Eleanor's shoulder bag. Eleanor had shrugged off the strap of her bag while falling across the top of the wall and fighting to find purchase against the wind and the chasm next to her.

That's when she saw the glitter of the emerald-and-diamond ring on the woman's finger as Angeline clutched the shoulder bag strap as if it was going to slow her momentum. As if it would keep her from going over the wall.

Her scream filled the air for a few moments before it faded away in the wind.

Lying on the narrow edge of the wall, Eleanor froze, terrified to move. She didn't dare breathe, let alone look over the wall to the street all those floors below. She could feel the wind rushing up the twenty stories at her. She clung to the wall beneath her with both hands, still afraid she was going over.

She feared she would have stayed there if Willie hadn't grabbed her, pulling her away from the ledge and into his arms. "Ellie. Ellie," he kept saying as he held her tight against him. "You're all right. You're all right."

"Angeline?" She knew the moment she heard the scream. Still she glanced back. Angeline Carter was gone. Icy horror seized her. Angeline had gone off the roof. Her momentum had carried her over the wall beyond the rooftop to plummet to the street below—taking only Eleanor's shoulder bag with her.

She felt her legs give out. Willie carefully lowered her to the roof floor. Dropping down beside her, he pulled her to him with one arm as he dug out his phone. She watched him, still stunned, as he called 911. She heard him say, "There's been a shooting on the roof at the law office of…" He gave the address. "We're going to need an ambulance."

An ambulance? She pulled back to look at him, afraid he'd been shot again.

He repeated the address to the operator.

That was when she glanced past him and saw the body lying on the roof, yards from them, unmoving. The ambulance was for Vernon. The wind brought the sound of sirens from far below. She closed her eyes and leaned into Willie, her fingers gripping the soft cotton of his Western shirt. She breathed him in and began to cry.

Chapter Twenty-Five

Police Chief Landry rubbed a hand over the back of his neck. "I thought we were rid of you, cowboy. This time, you're going in a cell. You can't just keep coming back here like some Old West vigilante." He heard the alert on his computer that he had a call. He ignored it. "It was bad enough when you were out here wearing a badge." Another alert, also ignored, and another. The man's office door was flung open.

Two FBI agents burst in, flashing their credentials.

"We'll be taking this from here," the older of the two agents Willie had spoken with said. "Mr. Colt, if you'll come with me."

Landry put up a fight, but got nowhere before Willie was led down the hallway and out of the building. It was a short car ride to the FBI's regional office.

"Feel like we've been here before," the older agent, Frank Rice, said. "Going to need your statement. We already have Ms. Shafer's."

He told the agent how he'd had his doubts. "Angeline Carter didn't seem like the brains behind this. But once I knew Jonathan Asher was already dead before the explosion that killed Lowell Carter, and that the second body found after the warehouse explosion wasn't Vernon's, I knew it had to be her. She brought Asher in when her husband was starting up the business. He must have realized after Mattson's visit that Angeline was the one who hired Vernon to blow up the building and kill Zoey Bertrand. He must have made the mistake of thinking he could cash in on that knowledge." Willie shrugged. "I think that once Angeline started tying up loose ends, she couldn't stop."

"The loose ends being?" the younger agent asked.

"E.L. Shafer and Vernon Murphy. He'd done everything she'd asked of him, but now he had to go and so did his attorney." He saw the two agents exchange a look. "By the way, how is Vernon?"

"He'll live. Maybe even long enough to stand trial. We have him in protective custody. Thank you for not killing him."

Willie shrugged. It had been touch and go. "He almost killed me, but I'm sure he'll be able to answer any questions you have about Angeline and this whole mess."

"Will you be staying around Seattle?" the older agent asked.

He shook his head. "No offense, but I'll be heading back to Montana after I take care of some personal business here." He rose, put his Stetson back on his head and started toward the door.

"I think it would be best if you stayed out of Seattle," the younger agent said. "You seem to have gotten on the wrong side of the chief of police. I wouldn't even jaywalk in this city if I was you."

Willie nodded. "Thanks for the advice. I was think-ing the same thing myself." He'd worn out his welcome in the big city and that, too, made it hard to finish what he'd started here.

ELEANOR LOOKED AROUND the long conference table at the men gathered there. She knew this meeting had been coming for some time and yet she could feel her parents' disapproval as well as Phillip McNamara's.

"Thank you all for being here," she said as she stood and cleared her voice. "As you all know, my parents were founding attorneys at this firm. Upon their death they put senior partner and managing attorney Phillip McNamara in charge. I now have that position."

A couple of the attorneys moved restlessly. Others stared at her, appearing half-afraid of what she was going to say.

She knew what she wanted to say, but she couldn't walk away that easily. "There are going to be some changes. For starters, we're actively going to hire more female and diverse attorneys. I'll be staying in charge of the firm until the changes are implemented and I can manage things with an occasional in-office visit. That means some of the other senior partners are going to have to step up."

"You're leaving the firm?" one of them asked.

"Not leaving. I'll still be keeping track of what's happening here—just not from the managing partner's office down the hall. I have a list of potential candi-dates whom I'd like to see in this firm. I'll be sitting in on final interviews."

She looked around the boardroom and saw resignation as well as disfavor.

"We don't really need any personnel other than replacing you and Phillip," one of the senior partners said.

"I'll be offering some suggestions on replacing several of the attorneys recently brought into the firm," she said. Phillip had liked it being an all-boys club. She thought of her mother, who would have done exactly what Eleanor was doing.

With that, she adjourned the meeting, walking out. She could hear the murmur of disapproval from some but nods from others. She smiled. Almost losing her life upstairs on the roof had made her even more determined to live the rest of her life on her terms.

When she reached her office, she found Willie Colt standing at her windows, Stetson dangling from his hand, his gaze on the city stretched out in front of him.

WILLIE TURNED AS he heard Ellie come into her office. She didn't seem surprised to see him. He watched her move to her desk, put down the folder she'd been carrying and face him.

"Did we have an appointment?" she asked.

He smiled at that and, tossing his hat on one of the chairs, moved around her desk. She turned toward him as he approached. He stopped within inches of her. "We have some old business we need to take care of." She raised an eyebrow but said nothing. They hadn't seen each other since what went down on the rooftop. "I left here once before without you, determined to put you and this city behind me. I'd watched my brothers fall in love." He winced. "And while it turned out fine after a time, it looked like pure hell at first. I saw the pain of falling in love and I wanted nothing to do with it."

Her gray eyes locked with his own as she waited.

"I was afraid that if I told you how I felt, you'd tell me you didn't feel the same," he continued. "But more than anything, I just didn't see how this could work between us. You this big-city lawyer, me a former deputy now running for sheriff. Our lives couldn't be more different. Until recently, I was a rodeo cowboy living on the road in my horse trailer camper and you a successful attorney living in a high-rise penthouse apartment. Not to mention we live in different states. You see the problem?"

"When you put it that way, I do," she said. "So, what solution did you come up with, former rodeo cowboy turned candidate for sheriff?"

He reached out and took her shoulders in his calloused hands. As he did, he noticed that while she was wearing a suit that he knew cost more than his horse, the top button of her silk blouse was undone and so was the next one. He met her gray gaze and couldn't help but smile. *In for a penny, in for a pound*, he thought. The one thing he wasn't doing was walking away again until he told her how he felt.

ELEANOR HELD HER BREATH. She could see the answer in his blue eyes, but she still needed, more than anything, to hear the words.

"I'm in love with you." He shook his head as if he couldn't believe he was finally saying it. "I love you and I want you and I'm damned sure going to do whatever I have to so we can be together."

She let out the breath she'd been holding. She shook her head. "I've been waiting for you to say those words. I was worried you never would."

He nodded. "Me, too."

She smiled. "I love you, too, Willie Colt." She felt the tension leave his hands holding her shoulders.

He let out a laugh. "Damned if I can stand being away from you. You're all I've thought about. I've tried to forget you." His hands moved from her shoulders to cup her face. A calloused thumb moved slowly over her lower lip, his gaze following the motion. Then he leaned forward and kissed her, pulling her into his arms as if he was never letting her go.

The kiss was full of promise, full of desire and passion, full of the love she'd seen in his eyes, heard in his words. She leaned into him, filled with glorious emotions. She'd missed him so much and had begun to believe that she'd never see him again. But then he'd rushed to Seattle to save her.

He drew back, still holding her as he looked into her eyes and asked, "What are we going to do?" His voice, so full of emotion, touched a chord inside her.

So much had happened up on that rooftop. She'd come close to dying, all the other near misses nothing compared to lying on that short wall, clinging to life. How could she have not made some big decisions about the rest of her life after that?

"Well," she said, the effects of the kiss still raging

through her bloodstream. "There is only one thing we can do."

"If you want me to move to Seattle, I will," he blurted out.

She laughed, shaking her head. "I've already made arrangements so I only have to come to Seattle to take care of business a few times a month. The firm is mine, I now have controlling interest."

"But what about your life here?" he asked. "Your apartment?"

"I'll keep it for when I have to come out." She reached for his face, cupping it in her hands. "As for my life? The only life I want is with you. But there is one thing you should know. My parents left me more than the firm. I'm rather…wealthy. Is that a game changer?"

He began to laugh, throwing back his head, before settling his gaze on her again. "I guess this means we won't have to live in my horse trailer camper," he joked. "I own Colt Ranch with my brothers. If this sheriff gig doesn't work out, I was thinking about buying some cattle and making it a real ranch. There's a spot on the land that I thought would be perfect for a house over-looking the river. But if you don't want to live that close to my kin—"

She silenced him with a finger on his lips. "After meeting Lori and James, I know I'm going to adore all of your brothers and their wives. I'd love to build on the ranch. Remember? I'm an only child without any family. I've already fallen in love with some of yours. Just the thought of raising our children so close to their cousins…" She stopped and met his gaze. "You do want kids, don't you?"

He drew her close. "I can't wait to make babies with you, Ellie. Or do you want me to call you Eleanor?"

Laughing, she said, "I kind of got used to Ellie. At least the way you say it."

He kissed her again, then pulled back. "My brother James gave me something." He reached into his jacket pocket and pulled out a small velvet box. She felt her heart jump. "I thought he was delusional offering me Grandmother's ring. I wasn't even sure you'd have me, let alone that we could work out a living arrangement."

Willie looked from the box to her as he dropped down on one knee. "E.L. Shafer, will you marry me?"

"She said yes?" James let out a hoot that brought Lori hurrying in from the kitchen as he put down his phone. "Willie asked Ellie to marry him, and she said yes." He saw Lori's eyes fill with tears and moved to take her in his arms. "You called it. When I gave him our grandmother's ring, he looked at me as if I'd lost my mind. I think he was afraid that she didn't feel the same way he did."

"I knew that she would say yes, if the darned fool ever got around to asking her." Lori hugged him and stepped back. "She's going to be my sister-in-law. When is the wedding? Where will it be?" As if seeing that her husband hadn't asked, she shook her head. "Men, you never ask the right questions. I have to call Bella and Carla. This is so exciting. Then I'll call Ellie and find out." She rushed from the room.

James smiled to himself, happy for his older brother. He'd never thought Willie would ever take that leap, but he was glad it was with someone like Ellie. He wished as he often did that his father was here to see this. All of them back at the ranch, all of them happy and married. Del would have loved having grandchildren.

He brushed away the regret, glad that things had worked out for Willie. They were going to have a great Christmas this year with all of them at home. His son would be born by then, his daughter old enough to be tearing into the presents under the tree. This was how it should be, he thought, family all together.

As he picked up the phone to call his brothers, he thought about what Willie had found in their father's wrecked pickup. The girl's necklace with the name DelRae engraved on it. Willie was right. They had to find out whom it had belonged to.

He hadn't wanted to get his brothers' hopes up, but he knew that once Willie and Ellie's wedding was over and they were settled in, it would be time for Colt Brothers Investigation to dig deeper into their father's death. Until they found out the truth, it would always hang over them. They had to make sure they got justice for the father who'd raised them.

THE WEDDING WAS planned for fall on the river not all that far from the property where Willlie and Ellie's house was under construction. It was a beautiful autumn day, the Montana sky a clear blue, the river sparkling in the sunlight and golden leaves fluttering on the nearby aspens.

Eleanor stood in front of the full-length mirror at Bella and Tommy's lodge. All around her were the women she'd come to love like sisters. She felt enveloped in this warm, loving family. Her three soon-to-be sisters-in-law were her matrons of honor. They'd been fussing over her all morning, often all four of them brought to tears of happiness.

"I really thought Willie would be the Colt who never married," Bella said as she straightened Eleanor's veil. "I know he felt responsible for his brothers after they lost their father. Mr. Tough Guy."

"The strong, silent type," Lori agreed. "He always took on more than he should have. But once James quit the rodeo and got the investigation business going, I think Willie realized that he didn't have to worry about his brothers as much."

"He was never going to marry," Carla said, and turned to Ellie. "Until he met you. You can't believe how miserable he was when he came back from Seattle. We could all tell that it wasn't the gunshot wound that was hurting him. It was leaving you."

Her sisters-in-law all agreed. "The problem was he's a Colt, stubborn as a post," Bella said, making them laugh.

"A post?" asked Lori. "I think the expression is as dumb as a post."

"That, too, sometimes," Bella said. "Dumb as a post when it comes to love. Look at Tommy. I swear he took his sweet time getting around to asking me to marry him."

"Davy, too," Carla agreed. "How awful is it that it

takes a near-death experience to get these men to realize that they can't live without us?" They all laughed and looked at each other.

"Now we get to raise our children together," Bella said, giving Ellie a hug.

There was a tap at the door. "We're ready for you," James announced through the door.

Eleanor went to the second-story window and looked out. She found Montana breathtaking, but nothing warmed her heart like seeing Willie all decked out in his Western attire, waiting to marry her by the river. Tears of joy burned her eyes. She bit them back as she gave thanks. What would her parents have thought about her marrying a cowboy and newly elected sheriff?

The thought made her smile as she turned back to the women who'd become the family she'd always longed for. "Let's do this," she said.

Eleanor couldn't wait to marry Willie Colt. She felt a rush of happiness. She'd found a real home and a real cowboy to curl up next to every night. She had to be the luckiest woman alive as she walked toward Willie and their bright, beautiful, loving future.

* * * * *

Watch for New York Times *bestselling author
B.J. Daniels's next Colt Brothers Investigation
novel, coming out May, wherever
Harlequin Books are sold.*

COMING NEXT MONTH FROM

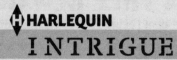

INTRIGUE

#2139 RIDING SHOTGUN
The Cowboys of Cider Creek • by Barb Han
Family secrets collide when Emmerson Bennett's search for her birth mother exposes her to the Hayes's cattle ranching dynasty. But Rory Hayes's honor won't allow him to abandon the vulnerable stranger, even when she puts him and his family in the line of fire...

#2140 CASING THE COPYCAT
Covert Cowboy Soldiers • by Nicole Helm
Rancher Dunne Thompson spent his adult life trying to atone for his serial killer grandfather. But redemption comes in the form of mysterious Quinn Peterson and her offer to help him catch a copycat murderer. They make an unexpected and perfect team...until the deadly culprit targets them both.

#2141 OVER HER DEAD BODY
Defenders of Battle Mountain • by Nichole Severn
Targeted by a shooter, single mom Isla Vachs and her daughter are saved by the man responsible for her husband's death. Adan Sergeant's vow of duty won't be shaken by her resentment. But falling for his best friend's widow could be deadly...or the only way they get out alive.

#2142 WYOMING MOUNTAIN HOSTAGE
Cowboy State Lawmen • by Juno Rushdan
Within moments of revealing her pregnancy to her coworker with benefits, FBI Special Agent Becca Hammond is taken hostage. Agent Jake Delgado won't compromise his partner's life—or their unborn child. But will he risk an entire town's safety just to keep them safe?

#2143 OZARKS MISSING PERSON
Arkansas Special Agents • by Maggie Wells
Attorney Matthew Murray's younger sister is missing and Special Agent Grace Reed is determined to find her. But when the case looks more like murder, both are drawn into a web of power and deceit...and dangerous attraction.

#2144 CRIME SCENE CONNECTION
by Janice Kay Johnson
Journalist Alexa Adams is determined to expose every bad cop in the city. But when danger soon follows, she's forced to trust Lieutenant Matthew Reinert. A man in blue. The enemy. And the only one willing to risk everything to keep her—and her mission—safe from those determined to silence her.

HARLEQUIN
PLUS

Try the best multimedia subscription service for romance readers like you!

Read, Watch and Play.

Experience the easiest way to get the romance content you crave.

Start your **FREE TRIAL** at
<u>www.harlequinplus.com/freetrial</u>.